CHILL
FACTOR

CHILL FACTOR

A Novel By

Christopher Knopf

BearManor Media

2015

Chill Factor

© 2015 Christopher Knopf

For information, address:

BearManor Media
P. O. Box 71426
Albany, GA 31708

bearmanormedia.com

Typesetting and layout by John Teehan

Published in the USA by BearManor Media

ISBN—1-59393-816-0
978-1-59393-816-1

FROM THE JOURNAL OF ELINOR BARRY

I DON'T KNOW the right thing to do. I don't even know the right thing to try to do. You're afraid of what you want, and yet you're afraid of what's right. You think back over those thoughts and you think how can you have these feelings? What kind of therapist are you? Inside these walls you do the best you can with what you're given. It is not my job to keep long term custodial facilities full. It is my job to prevent it, to determine manufactured delirium from genuine insanity. I didn't get into this business to play God. We use scientific analysis and statistics to say what we want to say. But we never admit that often we really don't know. But we do it. Because we can do it. Never mind that science has gotten ahead of humanity. What happens when suffering over-whelms the law? But that's not our directive. Insanity or balance. Only what if its beyond either choice? What if it's something so beyond definition that neither applies? Only tell me something. Why should he be allowed sanctuary when his actions were so monstrous.

DAY ONE

CLIMBING INLAND ALONG California's Central Coast Highway north of San Luis Obispo, past vineyards and ancient oaks and cattle dotting hillsides, she slowed. The cut-off was easy to miss. Taking it, a two lane road winding through greening hills, she saw from a distance the outlines of low-lying beige colored buildings, backed by the Coastal Range, giving the appearance at first glance of a research complex, or a campus. A large whitewashed concrete block at the side of the road with etched lettering dispelled that.

SANTA RITA STATE HOSPITAL

Further on, double lengths of ten-foot-high chain link fencing, topped by coils of razor wire encircling the facility, made clear whom it housed.

Braking her Prius at the gated entrance kiosk, she handed her identity to the uniformed guard.

"Elinor Barry. I've an appointment with Dr Fogel," she said.

The guard accepted her identification, checked it against his manifest, looked her over. Thirty-eight, he guessed, dressed professionally in conservative suit, subtly elegant, lacking artifice.

"May I see those, please" he said, but she was already ahead of him, handing over her purse and the large manila envelope on the passenger seat beside her.

Opening the purse, he rummaged through it, looked inside the envelope, nodded, returned both to her.

"If you'd pop the trunk, please."

She did so from the dash board. Glancing inside, he found it empty, closed the trunk. Slipping a parking permit under her windshield wiper, he returned her identity card along with a clip-on glycine covered tag.

"If you'd wear this, Doctor. Reception is at the end of the road. Any parking space marked visitor."

Navigating the circular lawn with its American flag protruding from its center like a putting green flag, Elinor found a parking space, cut the engine, left her car, purse and envelope in hand. She looked about. No one. Nor was it likely there would be. The word "trustee" was not in the hospital's lexicon. Turning to the building, she mounted the steps and entered.

"Wait here, please," the receptionist said behind the barred window, leaving Elinor to find a seat in the outer room.

Three clusters of people were waiting with her, not unusual for a Saturday. One, she saw, was a middle aged couple, the man in expensive coat and tie, designer jeans and English loafers, no socks, the woman in a Prada dress, pill box hat and dark glasses, their embarrassment at being there such they would meet no one's eyes. The second was a Mexican family, mother, father, pre-teen son lost in his Game Boy, all three dressed in clean but worn work clothes, conversation in Spanish totally dominated by the woman who kept up an accusatory stream at her husband. The third, Elinor was sure, was an attorney, hurriedly scribbling notes on a legal pad.

"Dr Barry?"

He stood in the doorway, wearing the blue fatigues of a nurse's attendant. He was more than that. Six-three, two hundred forty pounds, thickly muscled, he was clearly someone not to mess with, which was the point. He wore a staff identification tag. It said simply, WALTER.

Rising from her chair, purse and manila envelope in hand, she followed him through the door that closed with an electronic lock behind her. Without conversation he led her down a wide bare corridor, past numbered but unnamed office doors. From somewhere, far off in the bowels of the complex, a sudden wail, heart wrenching, full of loss and yearning, answered instantly by a cacophony of unintelligible multiple human mockery. It was not her first time there. Nor the first time she'd heard a cry of human sorrow. Her expertise, her training was to accept it, penetrate it, understand it. It was something she had never learned to reconcile. Reaching a door at the end of the corridor, the attendant rapped once, thrust open the door at the sound of "Come" from within, stepped aside for Elinor to enter.

"Elinor!"

"Hello, Aaron."

The office she'd been ushered into was small with organized clutter. There was a desk with chair, a couch, a bookcase filled with technical and medical volumes and manuals. A barred window looked out on a work-out area where a dozen men in short sleeve tan shirts and pants were being put through exercises. Rising from behind his desk, a slow smile spreading his face at her entrance, was Dr Aaron Fogel. It was a good face, a touch seamed at fifty, appealing, ingenuous.

"You're a welcome sight. How was the drive?"

"California in April? How can you miss?"

"Sit. Sit down. I've got you in at the Breakers. It's the best I could do."

"I didn't prepare for a stay."

"We're on a budget, and Sacramento's chewing away at that," he said, ignoring her pullback. "By the way, I'm sorry."

"What?"

"Your divorce."

"If two people aren't balancing on a seesaw, one has to move closer to the other. We never did."

"Again, I'm sorry," he said.

"Aaron…" There was impatience in her voice. Both knew he was stalling.

"Before you say no, you've read his file?" Aaron asked, nodding at the envelope she'd placed beside her on the couch.

Elinor rose, crossed to the window, looked out on the exercising men. They worked out silently, under tight control of watchful attendants.

"How'd you get him transferred here?" she asked.

"Truth? Four hours before the Board of Prison Terms begging for limited observations. But it's a short clock."

"What have you found?"

"Nothing helpful. No talking to himself, no making threats or lists, no scratching at walls or rolling around the floor like a psychotic idiot."

"That's not helping himself."

"Prison officials haven't released any more information than what you've read. I think that's all they have."

"What *do* we know about him?"

"I called his university. Universal agreement. Highly respected academic, kind, well-mannered, benign."

"Now, look…"

"I know. Before I push you into a corner…"

"You've got a staff."

"Of limited analysts."

"Why limited?"

"We're in the midst of transition, like the state's other mental hospitals, contending with an exodus of experienced people to higher paying prison jobs. What's left, well, you can imagine."

"What's their assessment?"

"He's a stone wall. They've tried everything they know. Bullied, badgered, seduction. They've thrown in the towel. The Inyo County DA's office wants answers and they want them quickly. They're proceeding with an indictment whether he chooses to cooperate or not. I think he belongs here. He's scheduled to be arraigned on the tenth in Inyo County. That's a week from Monday. We've got nine days to make a case for criminal insanity before the arraignment. It's his one chance."

"You know what you're up against."

"The M'Naghten rule."

"'The inability to know the nature and quality of the act, and to know the act was wrong.' You think you've got that here?"

"Under the irresistible impulse standard…"

"Good luck with that."

"I want to try."

"Aaron, for God's sake…"

"I know. The odds."

She turned, studied him closely.

"Why are you so invested in this?"

"He's not a rich man. It's going to be public defenders unless I can go to his law school and get pro bono representation. Also they have some heavy weight physiologists in his department who could give expert testimony on his behalf. But they're going to need validation."

"That's not what I asked."

"Something's amiss. He's the least likely candidate for what he did. It makes no sense."

"Our prisons are *full* of least likely candidates, Aaron."

"You haven't met this one."

"Why me?"

"If this is where he should be…" quickly adding parenthetically, "I don't think he'll expect a woman, it just might push him off course…"

"Hell of an endorsement."

"…he won't pull the wool over your eyes."

The room she was brought to was small, ten by eight and windowless. There was a plain wooden table with two facing chairs. There was a single overhead light and that was all. No pictures, cabinets, shelves, not even a carafe of water, nothing to distract the one under interrogation. The door opened, Elinor turning as Walter, ushered him into the room.

His name she knew from his file, academic achievements, age, employment. The rest? A sandy-complexioned man, hair turning grey, she saw, in short sleeve establishment suntans, average height, average appearance. She searched for more, could find nothing more. As much as he had blocked communication, he blocked disclosure. He stood manacled, hands and ankles.

"Hello." She offered her hand, quickly pulled it back realizing his shackles precluded his shaking hands with anyone. "My name is Elinor Barry. I'm a doctor. Won't you sit down."

He made no move to do so, did not even appear to have heard. Elinor, still standing, opened the file.

"That is your full name?" she began. "Doctor Frank Enari?"

No answer.

"You are forty-eight years-old," she said, sliding onto a chair at the desk as she turned to his file. "Not married. You are under employment at the University of California at Davis, tenured co-chairman of the Department of Physiology where you've been for the past sixteen years, is that right?"

Still no response. He remained standing, seemingly lost in another world. She turned to Walter.

"Take off his shackles."

Walter looked startled.

"It's my responsibility," she said.

The attendant hesitated, did as told.

"Wait outside, please."

Walter's eyebrows raised in a show of disagreement.

"Outside, thank you," she said.

Manacles in hand, Walter turned to the door, looked back, saw there was no appeal, went through the door, closed it behind him. The event appeared to bring Enari out of his stupor. He rubbed his wrists, looked at Elinor, a hostile child awaiting discipline, she saw, yet masking a terrible inner pain.

"How are you feeling?" she asked.

"A normalization of the word to feel," he answered, "first used in the English language to describe the physical sensation of touch through either experience or perception."

"Which applies to you?" she asked.

"Psychologically? The subject experience of emotion."

"That wasn't my question."

"Phenomenology and heterophenology are philosophical approaches that provide some basis for knowledge of feelings."

Elinor turned to the door.

"Guard!"

Enari's head came up on that as Walter reappeared. Enari looked at Elinor who gestured him toward his chair.

"Doctor?" she said. It was more than an invitation. It was a statement that said 'I am not here to suffer fools. I have a plate that's full and I'm that close to walking out that door and getting back to it.'

Enari sat, Walter retreating at a gesture from Elinor.

"I'm not your adversary, Doctor Enari," she said. "Not as we start. I can become that, or your advocate. Do you understand that?"

"My training is the art of understanding," he answered.

"This is not an art," she countered. "It is a competency evaluation. Do you understand the difference?"

"I learned at an early age what it is to be helpless," he answered.

"Is that what you feel?"

"Feelings again. Treacherous things."

"Doctor," and there was reprimand in her voice, "we can play this musical chairs 'til midnight."

"All those evasive inquiries."

"Then let me be specific. How did this happen?"

Enari sat back, silent. Elinor waited, then, no warning, rose, started to gather her things.

"Still," Enari said quickly, "it would be impractical not to allow ourselves some degree of indulgence."

Elinor looked back, eyebrows raised. He'd walked into it, trapped by his own condescending cleverness. But it gave her an opening. Still, she projected ambivalence, to leave, to stay. She lowered to her chair again. Her tone, when she spoke, suddenly softened.

"I was not always a therapist, Doctor," she began. "I was a teacher at first, Special Ed, fourth and fifth grade, nine and ten year olds. I had a student, Peter, big for his age, no motivation as a student, his parents, of course, blaming the school. But well enough behaved. He liked me. He'd stay after sometimes, help me clean up when the others were gone. Then one day he went berserk, scattered the other students, who were terrified, lashed out at me, struck me in the chest. I was in the hospital three days with a cracked rib. But he was the one in terrible pain. They expelled him, sent him to juvenile hall. I wanted to help him. They never let me try."

Whatever Enari expected to hear this wasn't it. He stared at her, no words coming to him to refute or deflect.

"All I know," he heard her saying, "is you need me badly."

"What is it you want?" he asked.

"I want to know how it began?"

TOWER MOUNTAIN

THE PHONE CALL, the hurried assemblage of documents, medical examinations, packing? Where *had* it begun? Their arrival. It seemed to start with that. White Mountain Road, northeast of Bishop in California's eastern Sierras. The pick-up flashing across the Owens River, toward the White Mountain Range rimming the eastern wall of Owens Valley. Three bags were in the pickup's open bed, two unmatching suitcases and a leather two suiter.

It was cold, freezing cold, late January, Enari remembered, seated in the cramped rear jump seat, staring out at the barren landscape racing by. Dressed in heavy outdoor clothing, very new, just bought, a briefcase with its raft of files in his lap, Enari was far more self-revealing than Elinor would later encounter. Meticulous, precise, very set in his ways, he was a careful man, geniality the salient characteristic, keenly practical, with a heart that imagination seldom warmed. Order was his security. And work, at which he was tireless. But for the moment his eyes held with tense concern on the speedometer settled in at eighty.

Up front with the driver sat Dr Robert Jones, Enari's academic and research partner of a dozen years, mid-forties, also dressed in heavy rough clothing. There the similarity ended. Handsome, with a seductive charm, he was very difficult to analyze, his eyes expanding from cynicism to sudden wide-eyed wonder that could make one sense he was joking. With a quicker mind than Enari, ideas flashed across his face like a meteor, a sudden brilliance, seldom maintained, that could just as quickly turn to distraction and boredom. Unlike Enari, he had no liking for analysis, the countless hours and days that went into collating data. His excitement came from discovery.

Enari looked back from his jump seat, through the cab's rear window, at the retreating snow-capped Sierras well behind them, when a sudden jar of the vehicle shook his sensibilities. He turned, looked ahead. Jones was looking too. The road had turned from asphalt to dirt, the pick-up fast approaching several low-lying buildings and trailers surrounded by fencing, the complex located off the base of the fast approaching eastern range. When all at once they were passing something on their right: a warehouse, set off by itself, made of corrugated aluminum with a sloping roof. Two men were pushing a three-place, 1100-pound-payload turbo charged helicopter, riding on wheels below its snow pontoons, out onto a concrete pad as the pick-up slowed in its own boil of dust, turned through entrance gates, past a sign that read:

HEADQUARTERS.
TOWER MOUNTAIN RESEARCH STATION.
ELEVATION 4,100

The room Enari and Jones were ushered into, the station's operation's center, owned desk, a couple of chairs, a single window facing north. Looking about they saw there was a radio with a transmission recorder, shelves piled high with blue-jacketed manuals and reports, a couple of oxygen tanks, and some unopened, undistributed boxes of varying supplies, mostly medical, when the door opened and Dr Ryan Horner entered quickly. Tower Mountain Station Director, he was, at thirty-eight, a first rate administrator and physiologist, looked like a lumberjack, full brown beard, wore laced-up boots, had a boyish weathered face that clearly acknowledged the depth of his concern. Extending his hand first to Enari, then Jones, he wasted no time, no words.

"Doctor Enari, I'm Doctor Ryan Horner."

"Doctor," Enari greeted him.

"Robert Jones," Jones offered.

"I'm going to lay this on you fast," Horner said. "There's coffee."

Enari waved him off. Jones indicated he'd get his own.

"They tell you anything at the University?" Horner continued.

"They said there was an emergency," Jones answered lightly. "You volunteered us."

"I'm going to put you up on the mountain," Horner said. "I need you there three months."

There was a silence.

"For what?" Jones asked.

Horner studied Jones for a moment. He'd met Jones before, he was sure of it.

"Houston, wasn't it?"

"Four years ago," Jones nodded.

"The Brain Drain," Horner recalled. "Fifteen hundred scientists brought together from forty centers of research to help send three men past the moon. Sorry. Our part in that all comes down to you."

Enari looked at Jones, then back at Horner.

"Doctor, we've completed our research…"

"Controlled Experiments On Laboratory Animals," Horner said, picking a manual off his desk. "Inducing Behavioral Disorders Well Recognized In Man. By Jones and Enari."

"Exactly," Enari said.

"Our program *is* your research, Doctor," Horner said, dropping the manual back onto the desk. "Exactly."

Enari's interest was suddenly piqued. Jones turned, coffee poured, eyebrows arched in question.

"We're probing the effect of stress situations given limited atmosphere with respect to interplanetary flight. It's in a nascent stage but it's coming." Horner's voice was hurried as though time was against him. "We've guaranteed to deliver our findings by April tenth. That's the outside date. We've ninety days."

"Working with what?" Jones asked.

"We've established a colony of monkeys. Pigtails and chimps. You'll be taking another one in under sedation. Some have been up there three and four years. This one will give you a point of comparison."

"Who's operating the facility now?" Enari asked.

"I'm not that sure that anyone is," Horner answered.

Enari and Jones stared.

"Say again," Jones said.

"We put a man in there in late November, six weeks ago for the winter. Howard Vogel?"

The two men nodded, respecting the name.

"I asked for a team," Horner went on, "We're tight on budget, they went with one man. He's an old hand, he's been there before. It wasn't a good idea. Two weeks ago he began to grow squirrely. Radio calls irregular, less and less articulate, then irrational."

"Squirrely," Jones repeated.

"He reported one day he'd spent the night in conversation with Alexander the Great, okay?" said Horner. "The next day he was fearful and guarded."

Jones turned, moved to the window, lit a cigarette from a lighter retrieved from his pocket, stared up at the mountain.

"Four days ago we got this."

Horner activated the recorder. His voice came through, anxious, pressing.

"Summit Laboratory. Base to Summit..!"

A man's voice broke in, hysterical over static.

"Oh, God, please, please..!"

"Bishop Station. Base to Summit..!"

"Get me out! You don't know! Get me out..!"

"Base to Summit! Do you receive..?"

"God, please!" Desperate, pleading. "Don't you see what's *happened*? Oh, God..!"

When the voice transmission went dead. Nothing but static.

Horner cut off the recording.

"That was it," Horner said. "Nothing more. We've tried every hour for the past four days. A radio breakdown? Maybe. We don't know. Some of our transmittal equipment's relatively primitive but it's always been serviced and worked. The wind kept us from getting up there, then there was snow. It broke this morning. We're going to send you in and bring him out."

Still at the window, Jones nodded up at the mountain.

"Hallucination and paranoia," he said. "A psychotic combination."

"You're at fourteen thousand feet there, Doctor," Horner explained with a touch of impatience. "Only four thousand feet below the limit at which man can survive without life support systems. Which is the point of our work. I've brought out Nobel physiologists who couldn't add two and two. That isn't psychotic, it's phobic. Cabin fever and damn thin air. He'll be alright when I get him down. It's those monkeys that worry the hell out of me. I don't know if he's doing workups, recording his work. I don't even know if he's feeding them. If he isn't, it's four years work down the drain. The delay'll kill our part in it."

Enari uncapped his pen to take notes.

"What *are* the workups?"

"Controlled inducement of any form of stress man might encounter in prolonged confinement. Hunger, panic, fear." He slid a folder toward Enari. "It's all in there, along with house rules." He nodded at Jones cigarette. "That's the last one of those. No smoking, no liquor. Not at that elevation. Collate your data for analysis, communicate once daily with me. Five at night. That's religion. Val Adams will fly you in. Wear these."

He pulled two cold weather coats from a hanging rack. They were knee-length, insulated with goose down, had adjustable, removable faux-fur hoods.

"We're sending up a new short wave in case," Horner concluded. "He'll show you how to operate it. Just get *in* there! Let me know we got something to work with! Wait here."

And he was gone. It had been unloaded on them like a ton of cement and it left them dazed. Particularly Enari. What he'd heard went to his head, like alcohol. He glanced at Jones. Taking a deliberate drag on his cigarette, Jones looked up at the mountain again, trapped and rankled by it. It was Enari who broke the silence.

"What do you think?"

"He sounds like some damn C.O.," Jones answered. "Jump and don't argue."

"We can't turn him down."

"Turn him down, hell. We're enlisted."

Twenty minutes later rotor blades whirled at a roar above the helicopter as it sat on its pad awaiting lift off. Inside, Enari and Jones adjusted shoulder straps as Val Adams, on assignment from the Space Authority, sat at the controls checking magnetos. All three wore crash helmets and were bundled in their cold-weather gear as Horner approached carrying a tranquilized chimpanzee in a small transporting cage barely large enough to accommodate it. Surgical tape, bearing its name and a number, was attached to the cage door. Glancing over his shoulder, west across the valley at the buildup of storm clouds above the Sierras, Horner reached inside, placed the cage between the feet of the two scientists strapped now into rear seats.

"New front building up," Horner warned over the engine's roar.

Adams closed the magneto switch, nodded. He was ready. Horner turned to the two scientists.

"All set?"

"Set," Jones answered for both of them.

Whipped by overhead wind from the idling rotors, Horner closed the Plexiglas door, withdrew. The copter's engine accelerated. For a moment it rested on its snow pontoons, heavily laden with equipment, supplies, luggage, men—then it was rising in a swirl of dust. It climbed straight up, seemed to hang midair, banked away quickly to the north east. Horner took a step toward the retreating copter, his face, no concealing it, filled with apprehension.

Aboard the copter the climb into and through the mountains was awesome. At 5,500 feet, the snowline. Working in and out of contours like the shoreline of a lake, 10,000 feet and nothing but white. Then above the pines. Rocks now, and few of those, no trees, a lunaresque landscape. Then over terraced ridges and flat barren plateaus, chased by their own shadow, elusive, darting over a ceaseless flow of snow.

Aboard the copter, no conversation. The toil of flight, the infinity of white too inhibiting. Enari's eyes dropped down to the caged chimp still under sedation. With the toe of his boot, he lifted the cage, brought the animal's face into view. The surgical tape across the cage read, 'Geronimo - #409.'

Enari stared with a sense of sympathy, lowered the cage, looked through the Plexiglas bubble. Tower Mountain loomed above them, the culminating point of a long narrow range, aloof and improbable, all pure white, a violent up thrust of granite and volcanic wrath. Sweeps and scarps of snow stretched away from the peak, the sun a dim orb, almost obscured now by formless mists and vapors.

Peering out the Plexiglas over Enari's shoulder, Jones mouth became a thin tight line as he stared, the superb arrogance of the place overwhelming.

"There is it," Adams nodded, shouting over the engine's throbbing roar.

Instantly Enari and Jones strained to see, seeing nothing but aching desolation, all movement ceased, nowhere a living thing, nothing but a sea of white, save for a dot coming into view in a shallow saucer on the saddle below the peak. The dot increased—and Summit Laboratory came into view, bleak and cold, half buried in snow, the copter angling, lowering toward it.

A tremendous spray of snow as it settled, pontoons touching, bouncing, then holding, like buoys on water. Adams cut the engine, the overhead rotors winding down, the three men looking through the Plexiglas bubble, seeing nothing at first but swirling white thrown up by the overhead blades, 'til, snow and rotors settling, the outlines of the Quonset hut began to emerge fifty feet away, sterile, weird, a forty-by-hundred foot structure, half buried in fresh winter snow so deep, so dry a man would sink to his waist without webbed shoes, so high in altitude he would give up after twenty yards even with them. Atop the hut a wind sock whipped in a quickening, bitter wind. A weather vane vacillated on its axis, its propeller spinning fitfully. A burst of snow whipped across the front of the copter, rattled icily off its bubble, momentarily receded, leaving the hut again in full view. A ghostly intrusion on a dead world, it offered no welcome.

Inside the copter no one had moved. Not even Adams. Enari glanced at him, saw him grim and set, started to look away, looked back, startled. Adams was reaching into a small tool box under his seat, was removing a .22 automatic and a nine-round clip fully loaded. Arming the weapon, Adams slipped it into his coat pocket, pulled his gloves up tightly, opened the cabin door to a blast of wind-swept ice.

Emerging, Adams stepped hip deep into bitter, sub-freezing cold. There was no beaten track to follow, it was all breaking trail and deadening labor. Steam pouring from his mouth, he half plowed, half crawled toward the Quonset hut entrance. Behind him Enari and Jones began to emerge from the copter themselves, Jones first. The shock of dropping hip deep into snow brought a gasp from Enari. Reaching back into the cabin, Jones acquired the caged chimpanzee, moved with Enari toward the hut. It was all pure struggle. For three or four steps they sank only to their knees, then to their hips once again. Steam hissed from their lungs, searing and painful. The altitude, the labor, the wind and cold brought exhaustion quickly.

Adams was the first to reach the entrance. The door was mostly protected from the elements by an overhang. The latch was exposed. Adams tried it, found it locked. Pulling off one glove, he dug for his keys, a half dozen, attached to a ring, selected the one wanted, tried to insert it. His bare hand was shaking so badly he had to cap it with his gloved one, finally jammed the key into the lock, tried to turn it. The lock was frozen. He slammed against it with his gloved hand, once, twice 'til it broke free. The key turned.

Inside the Quonset hut the door opened in, admitting Adams to a small dank vestibule. A litter stood against one wall. And a snow sled. There was a wide-mouth shovel, and there were snow shoes. Steam still pouring from his mouth, Adams blinked away snow blindness, looked about. Lights were on, along with the soft hum of a generator, and static, but it was very cold, freezing. Listening for other sounds, Adams heard nothing. He called out.

"Vogel?"

No answer. Behind him Enari and Jones straggled in, Jones with the anesthetized chimpanzee, Enari clutching their paper work, both men miserable, weak from their ordeal, the last of their strength exerted, gasping for air. Closing the door, Adams cautiously entered a corridor running left and right the length of the lower story of the two-story metal building, called out again.

"Vogel?"

Again no answer, the place beyond eerie. Moving in from the foyer, Jones and Enari drew up beside Adams, Enari with his hand thrust in his mouth, biting out ice which had clustered cruelly inside his glove between his fingers. The muscles in Jones' face were taut as wire cables.

Across from the entrance, they saw, was what appeared to be a combination kitchen-common room. It was in total disarray, food rotting, spilled on the floor. On a table stood a shortwave radio, turned on, emitting the static. Drawn to it, Adams picked up the microphone, pressed the transmittal button.

"Summit to base. How…now…brown…you picking this up?"

Horner's voice broke through.

"Clear as hell! What have we got?"

"Hold on," Adams said.

Adams lowered the mike, leaving it live as Jones and Enari entered from the corridor, a look of hopeful, hopeless query on their faces. Leaving them to the shock of their surroundings Adams moved back into the corridor as Jones slowly set down the cage bearing the still sedated chimp, looked about.

"Christ, what a battlefield," Jones said. "Look at this place."

As distressing as the disorder were the living and functional facilities. Stove, furniture, tables, utensils. If they weren't bought at garage sales, then junkyards. Food sat rotting in unwashed pots and pans.

In the corridor Adams reached the first of several doors opening off the corridor, paused.

"Vogel?"

No answer. He threw open the door. It was the shop room, fully equipped with hand and power tools for electrical, machine or mechanical repairs. Otherwise empty.

"Vogel? It's Val Adams. Vogel?"

Moving down corridor, Adams pushed open the next door, revealing the lavatory-shower room. A sink for hand washing and shaving, one toilet, one shower. Also a large basin for washing clothes, along with a portable drying rack. No Vogel.

In the kitchen-common room Enari circled the large table upon which the shortwave stood crackling, spotted something on the floor. Stooping down, he retrieved an eight by ten spiral backed note book. He opened it, leafed through its pages, frowned.

"What the hell?" he said.

Jones turned.

"What is it?"

"His journal."

Jones approached Enari who held out the book, took it, leafed through it himself, looked back at Enari in astonishment.

In the corridor Adams turned from the lavatory-shower room, moved on to the next, hesitated, opened the door to the physical work-up lab. Treadmills, isolation chambers. Nothing of Vogel.

The wet on his brow was from more than exertion. At the end of the corridor a stairway climbed to second floor living quarters. Off the stairway, at the end of the building, was a large glass-faced door. Approaching it, Adams' hand dropped toward the knob. It never got there as what he saw through the window glass brought a shout from his mouth.

"Down here! Down here!"

Jones and Enari broke from the kitchen-common room into the corridor, raced down it. Jones, the first to reach Adams, looked through the window.

"Jesus Christ!"

Throwing open the door Jones led Enari and Adams into the examination and housing room where the monkeys were maintained. Bright, overhead lights were full on. There was no sign of Vogel, but the monkeys, quartered in cages, out of water, out of food, appeared in deep distress, even trauma.

"They're freezing to death! Where the hell's the heat?" Jones shouted.

"In the hall!" said Adams, and he was gone.

"The keys to these cages!" Enari furiously snapped his fingers. "The keys! The keys!"

He found them himself, attached to a ring, hung on the wall. He grabbed them, moved to the cages. There were eight of them, six occupied, pigtail monkeys and chimpanzees, each with a fanciful name and a number in large block letters on surgical tape attached to their feeding doors: Napy, Julie, Genghi, Willie, Freddie, Allie. Corresponding numbers, taped to each of the keys, made access immediate. Quickly unlocking the first of the cages, Enari brought out Napy, a grey-furred pigtail in deep stupor.

In the corridor Adams emerged from the shop room, carried a can of fuel oil to Jones who was kneeling before a primitive fuel burning heater at the end of the corridor with a round metal chimney traveling up through the roof of the building. Jones knew what he was doing, had already removed the cap on the intake and opened the flue, impatiently reached for the can of fuel.

"I got it! Got it!"

Impelled by urgency, Adams left the heater to Jones, moved to the stairway, climbed the stairs, stopped as he reached the top.

"Vogel?"

The upper bay was a long, single room running the length of the building containing army-style bunks for as many as half a dozen. There was a library with a couple chairs, and a pool table. Books lay about, open and scattered. A single bed, the only one seemingly to have been occupied, was unmade. Clothes were strewn on the floor, rank and unwashed.

Adams stared, his breath increasingly labored. He turned, headed back down the stairs to the corridor where Jones, on his knees, capped off the fuel, pulled his cigarette lighter from his pocket, lit the heater.

Adams moved past him, back down corridor toward the far end of the building. Reaching another door just past the foyer, Adams stood before it, called out sharply, anger building in his voice.

"Vogel!"

He threw open the door revealing the medical and research laboratory, well equipped, and a shambles, glass on the floor from broken beakers, blood samples caking in test tubes, instruments, scattered about unsterilized.

Adams pulled back slowly, having reached the point of control beyond which he could not go unfortified. Few things frightened him, but he was frightened. He reached inside his coat pocket.

Down corridor Jones had fired the heater, opened it fully, looked up, reacted startled at what he saw. Adams had pulled out the .22 automatic. Slowly rising, Jones watched as Adams reached the far end of the building, flattened protectively. There was no door, this room was open

"Vogel?"

It was the generator room housing generator, water tanks and water-making apparatus. Nothing else.

Adams swallowed. He turned. Across the corridor a large metal door with a small unbreakable glass window led into the last unopened room in the building. Jones rose slowly, held by the .22 as Adams moved to the door. He did not call out. He reached down. His hand held on the knob, then turned it, threw open the door, stared in. For a moment Jones stood, trying to read Adams whose face seemed frozen in time. Moving down corridor, Jones reached him, moved to the door, looked inside.

It was the electronics room where weather-reading equipment, tape deck, an old fashioned tape recorder and computers were housed. The storm window was open, snow flowing in, piled deep on the floor. The room was frigid, far below freezing. Vogel sat, hunched over the tape recorder, microphone in hand, frozen to death.

The wind had increased, driving snow like wild locusts, biting Adams' face as he worked. Wearing snow shoes, he'd brought Vogel's body out on the litter, secured it to the snow sled, transferred the litter and Vogel to the helicopter's pontoon. Testing the straps, he satisfied himself they'd hold. He turned to the sled, piled with the last of the cargo to be brought inside, among it the replacement radio they'd brought with them. With quick high steps he towed the sled back to the building.

In the Quonset hut's examination and housing room, hot water was turned on full, run into a basin, the steam adding humid warmth to the rapidly rising temperature of the room. Enari, alone in the room, had removed his cold-weather gear, wore a white surgical coat and an anti-contamination mask. His right hand encased in a triple-ply glove with a long protective cuff, he carried Freddie, a still groggy chimpanzee, from a polished wooden examination table. The cage door squeaked audibly as he opened it, placed the chimp inside, locked the cage, unlocked the next and last, reached in.

The pigtail monkey, Allie, still not recovered enough to stand, had enough adrenalin flowing to show its disaffection for man. Broad chested, powerfully muscled, of more than ordinary size, its neck and shoulders a mass of bristling hair, the monkey clamped its teeth on the outstretched glove.

Enari pried the glove free, withdrew it, left the monkey inside, closed and locked the cage, stepped back, looked them over as he pulled off the glove. All done that could be done, for the while at least, he removed his mask, shut off the water, hung the ring of keys to their cages on a post across the room, moved out, leaving the monkeys to their recovery. Their cages had been cleaned, their water bottles filled. Still not free of the drowsiness and numbness brought on by the cold, food withheld for the while, they were like knocked-down fighters coming off the floor for whatever else was going to be thrown at them.

In the electronics room Jones, still dressed in his cold-weather gear, had been shoveling snow away from the storm window. The altitude and the urgency made it exhausting work. Slamming the storm window down, two times, three, Jones finally closed it, locked it against further snow and cold. He gasped for air, but the work was completed. The pile of snow left on the floor had yet to melt. He moved out.

In the kitchen-common room Adams, himself breathing heavily from his ordeal, was on the short wave radio. It was where they found it, operating properly, the spare brought up at Horner's direction set aside in a corner. Adams, his set of keys in his hand, had placed the .22 on top of the radio. In background Enari was occupied at a small corner table jotting notes on a clipboard, Vogel's journal on the table beside him.

"I don't know what the hell," Adams said into the mike. "You look—lab, the kitchen—he just took it apart. We found his journal. Nothing recorded the past three days. He must have been out of his mind the way he—we're on open channel , you want all this?"

"Where'd you find him?" Horner's voice came through.

"In the electronics room. It looks like a heart attack."

Jones entered from the corridor, peeled off his coat as Adams went on.

"He must have assumed he was locked in. He wasn't. The door was unlocked. I don't know what he did with his keys, they're missing, probably out in the snow somewhere when he was making water. He raised the storm window. God knows he knew better than that—I suppose to try and get out which makes no sense. That let the snow and the cold in. He must have got hit when he tried to close it. It's all I can figure. A heart attack's painful, there was pain on his face, just sitting there, frozen at the tape recorder, holding the mike. It looks like he ran off about three hundred feet of tape before he died. It'll probably tell you what he thought was happening."

Silence, a long one, nothing but static.

"I got fifteen minutes to get out of here," Adams said. "It's coming in pretty good."

"Let me talk to Jones and Enari."

"Here," Jones said.

"How are the monkeys?"

Enari rose with the clipboard, approached the short wave.

"I haven't checked them all," Enari explained. "but I think they're all right. Emerging from torpor. Pupillary signs responsive, no indication of distress or infection. They were out of food and water, but it couldn't have been for long. No indication of starvation or dehydration. Just cold. You got a break when the generator stayed on. There's a thousand watts of light in there, that issued some heat."

"What about Geronimo?" Horner asked.

"What? Oh."

Enari looked down. Geronimo had been removed from his transporting cage, half sat on a worn upholstered couch, groggily coming back to the living.

"Coming out of his drunk," Enari said.

"How bad is the physical damage?" Horner asked.

"It'll clean up," Jones cut in. "It's mostly disorder. We can work around the rest of it. Along with what we brought with us, we're okay on food. Plenty of canned and freeze dried."

"I'd like that tape recorder," Horner said.

"We'll need the recorder," Jones answered.

"We transcribe all our work," Enari added. "We never know when a thought can turn out to be vital."

"Can you remove the tape?" Horner asked. "Send it out with Val?"

"Everything in there's pretty damn cold," Jones argued. "It got down to twenty below. I can't even get a reading on the needles, the systems are frozen. That tape could splinter like a sheet of glass. We'll run it off as soon as it thaws, let you know what's on it."

"Do it right then, okay," Horner conceded, "let me know. Val?"

"Hello."

"Give them what orientation you can, then get out of there."

"Summit out," Adams said.

"Base out."

Adams was into his orientation the moment he flipped off the transmission key.

"Volume control, transmission key and power. You're open for two-way conversation. You've got the backup transmitter in case this crashes." He gestured. "Stoves are butane, tanks are stored in the generator room. Refrigerator's electric."

Adams moved into the corridor, Jones and Enari following. He stopped, pointed down corridor right to each of several doors.

"Two heaters. Controllable outlets. Refill every thirty-six hours. Fuel oil in the shop." He pointed. "Upper bay. Bunk room" He turned. "Generator and storage. I'll show you that one."

He moved quickly, the two men trailing, brought them to the generator room, took them from one fixture to another, pointing or slapping his hand against the facility.

"Generators. A primary with a backup system. Water storage tanks. Hot water tanks. Water making tank, you make your own water. Shovel snow in through that flap, into this vat. It's dry as hell so shovel plenty. Hot water circulates through this tank, comes out that nozzle, melts the snow. Open this valve, it's drawn off into those storage tanks. Whenever you get the weather, make water. Manuals are in the shop, they'll answer questions."

He hands his ring of keys to Jones.

"Keys."

The helicopter sat, rotors idling, the beginning of a snowfall bombarding the Plexiglas bubble.

In the medical and research lab, Jones moved slowly to the window, stared out. Through the window he could see the outline of the helicopter. There was the sound of the motor accelerating, gaining power. Snow scattered from the force of the whirling blades, the copter rose.

In the kitchen-common room, Enari, clipboard in hand, started toward the widow—suddenly saw Adam's .22 atop the shortwave radio. Picking it up, Enari moved to the window between the refrigerator and the stoves, looked out futilely, the gun in his hand as through the window the copter rose, banked sharply, swallowed by the oncoming snowstorm as it disappeared to the southwest.

Holding on the window 'til all that was left was the retreating sound of the copter's engine, Enari turned, the .22 still in his hand. He looked about. What to do with it? He settled on a kitchen drawer.

The wind had ceased. Snow was falling, but gently. Lights shone from within the Quonset hut. It was night.

In the examination and housing room the monkeys had reached nearly full recovery and had now been fed. Pacing back and forth in their cages, they were potency in motion, beasts not pets, restless and cheerless and grim.

In the kitchen-common room Geronimo was something else. Recovered from his sedation, the chimp was beset with anxiety. Pacing back and forth, he had yet to leave the couch where he had been placed hours ago, two feet to the left, two feet to the right, no less, no more, an upward thrust of his head each time he made a turn. Nor would he take food, not even when Enari held out a biscuit, trying to coax him, soothingly.

Alone in the kitchen with the chimp, Enari had cleaned and scoured the place. Pots and pans hung neatly above the stove. Food had been capped and restored, the rotted discarded. Dinner was over. From above there was the sound of pool balls colliding, followed by a long roll and a clatter. Reacting to the noise, Enari smiled wryly, picked up two cups of steaming coffee freshly made, moved out, clipboard tucked under his arm leaving Geronimo to his frustration.

In the upper bay Jones, stripped to his waist, wearing pajama bottoms only, fired a cross-table carom shot, sank the four ball as Enari came off the stairs carrying coffee and clipboard.

"You believe that?" Enari said, puffing heavily. "Just that climb. Dizzy as hell."

"Stick around 'til they open the glue," Jones answered.

Enari grinned, gulped air, placed a cup of coffee on the pool table's cushioned edge for Jones as Jones circled the table, lined up his next shot.

"Five ball in the corner pocket," Jones said.

"Not bad," Enari nodded, looking over the place. "Not half bad."

It was Enari's first sight of the living-recreation-study facilities and they exceeded his expectations. Primitive and bare though they were, the place was spacious. A corner library contained three hundred books and journals. And a library table. The bay had been superficially straightened by Jones, little more. Enari's two suitcases were thrown onto one bed, Jones two-suiter lay open on another. Still, to Enari, the place exuded a welcome warmth.

"I give it two stars," he said.

Still holding his own cup of coffee, still with the clipboard tucked under his arm, Enari tried one of the beds as Jones fired again, sank his shot.

"Not exactly posturepedic, but not that bad," Enari offered.

He looked at Jones who was circling back about the table, eyeing his next shot.

"What do you want to take?" Enari asked, consulting his clipboard.

"What do I want to take what?" Jones asked.

"Duty roster."

"*Duty* roster?"

"We've got to keep the place up," Enari explained, setting his coffee on a side table. "Clean out the cages, make water, fill the…"

"Three ball," Jones said, back to his game. "Basic isosceles."

He fired, a difficult shot, barely missed.

"Dead cushions," Jones assessed. "Try with the nine. Same principle. Soften the shot."

"Listen. We can break it up," Enari offered.

"What do I want to take," Jones said as he lined up the shot. "I'll take the water."

"You'll make water, you take the water." Enari wrote it down on his clipboard. "And the butane."

Again Jones' fired, made it.

"I'll fill—I'll fill the heaters," said Enari, making the notation.

"Eleven," Jones said, bending, squinting as he assessed his next shot.

"Who cooks?" asked Enari.

"You cook."

"Who cleans?"

"Oh, that's the guy that cooks."

"Now, wait…"

Jones fired again. He made it. With a rueful smile, Enari set down his clipboard.

"Do you mind a little business?" he said.

"Go."

"Okay. Did you notice Geronimo? Back and forth on that couch? He's been in a cage all his life, that's been his security. Take him out of the cage, he's filled with anxiety, restricts himself to the limits he's known. I'd like to play with that. Let him run loose. See how he adapts to being released from confinement."

"Fifteen off the one ball, in the corner," Jones said.

Enari's hand came down, covered the one ball, stopping the shot. Jones looked at him, a little startled.

"I like this up here, Robert. I like the work. I like having defined goals, when conclusions are drawn. I like analysis. You like to explore the unknown. I don't. I don't like going around corners, into places I can't see. You do. You like clues and what they all add up to. That's what's eating you, Robert, you haven't got a mystery to solve. All the work's been done for you. They've taken all the excitement out of it for you, they've done your job. But not mine."

Jones opened his mouth wide, stretching it into a yawn.

"Christ, this altitude," he said with a shudder—then set the pool cue down on the table. "Three months, baby, that's the sentence. Living in the hull of a capsized scow."

"Work with me," Enari pleaded.

Jones looked at his friend, saw the anticipation and hope in his face. With a deep sigh, Jones nodded his head in acquiescence, shook it in resignation.

"Insanity didn't get Vogel," he said. "He died of boredom."

DAY ONE CONTINUED

IN THE WINDOWLESS interrogation room Elinor reflected on the word. Insanity. How it's been coopted. Insane shape. Insane results. Insane sex. How had it come to mean unique, passionate, extreme. *Mens sano incorpore sano.* From a sound mind in a healthy body? In the medical profession the term was now avoided in favor of a diagnosis of specific mental disorder, the presence of delusion or hallucination. *Non compos mentis.* The decomposed mind.

She looked at Enari seated across from her. Until now his narrative had been straightforward.

"Tell me about that first night after Vogel," she said.

"I saw I could like it, if that's what you mean."

"Settled in."

"Yes."

"The spirit of the place..."

"Yes."

"Undisturbed by far off struggles," she probed.

Enari did not answer.

"What?" she asked.

Still no answer.

"What is it you have to tell me?"

"Doctor," he said, evading answer. "You called yourself a doctor. Medical? PhD?"

"It's my job to question."

"Married?"

"Doctor..."

31

"Married?"

She thought about whether to answer or not, decided to.

"I was."

He seemed to think that over.

"What was it like?"

"It?"

"Communication, affection, sex?"

"Why do you ask?"

"There was a student in my class. She was twenty. I was forty-five. I can't explain it, I was in love with her. She'd come into class sometimes, I could see the top of her breasts. I wanted to tell her how I felt, how could I? I fantasized a relationship. I dyed my hair. I'd go to sleep at night imagining I was making love to her. We had conversations in my mind. She was at the end of an affair, I imagined, and she came to me crying, and I'd hold her in my arms and she'd say, 'Why can't I find someone like you'..."

"What is it that happened that night on the mountain?" Elinor interrupted.

"Why would you assume that?"

"Because you don't want to talk about it."

INITIUM

THE MOON PLAYED in through narrow skylights in the curved metal ceiling of the Quonset hut, falling on Jones and Enari, asleep in their beds in the upper bay, Enari peacefully, not a muscle quivering. An unwonted calm was on his face. Two beds away Jones slept fitfully, rolled from his left side onto his right. But elsewhere there was the spirit of peace and quietude, of smooth pulsing life without violence, undisturbed by far-off struggles, the hum of the generator the only sound, constant, reassuring.

In the electronics room, cold, metallic, much was as Jones had left it. Moonlight splintered off the snow outside, streamed in through the storm window, kindling the room with sulfurous light. Computers and medical analyzers, automated machines for completing complex diagnoses, stood like bleak engines of action in repose. The storm window was locked shut.

On the floor, what snow Jones had left had now melted, so dry it left little water. On a six-foot long bench table stood the anemometer and electronic calculator. Beside them the tape recorder slumbered, squat and black and polished chrome. The spools were as before when found. The counter showed three hundred feet played out.

Suddenly, no warning, a click. A red light snapped on, bright and burning. With aroused acceleration the spools began to reverse, the counter with it, erasing the recording.

Jones, bundled in his cold weather gear, gasping desperately, shuddered in pain. His head was back, his eyes were dazzled by the late light of day. His mouth was opened wide, drawn back so tightly from his teeth, it seemed he had no lips at all. Breath steamed from his mouth in a wretched wheeze, his face, with its four day growth of beard, was nipped by cold to a gleaming pink, his lashes and eyebrows white with ice, the ear and neck flaps of his greatcoat matted with ice from frozen perspiration. He flung a glance toward towering Sierra minarets covered white far across the Owens Valley, reflecting the last of the sun. The sky was clear, the heavens brass. The day was worn out.

Swallowing back pain and fatigue that nearly crippled him, he lowered his head, picked up the shovel he'd been wielding, resumed the tortuous labor of scooping snow through the storm flap into the melting vat inside the Quonset hut.

In the generator room steaming hot water streamed from the high arching nozzle protruding from the hot water tank, melting snow piled to capacity in the large drum-like water-making vat. The sound of the generator all but drowned out the play of steaming water as Jones, the valve opened fully, still gasping from his efforts, turned and stumbled out, the water left running.

In the corridor Jones moved down past doors. As he moved, more nearly staggered, sucking air, he let his heavy weather coat slip from his shoulders, drop to the floor as he moved on, shirt soaked with perspiration. Reaching the lavatory-shower room, he pushed inside, made it to the sink, threw one arm out to support himself on the bowl, turned the water on full. There was a bandage on one of his fingers. Dropping his head under the stream, he let the water play over his hair, his face. Lifting his head, he turned off the water, held there, arms extended, head down, still gasping. He took down a towel, dried off his face, moved from the room with the towel.

In the physical workup lab Enari, dressed in a surgical coat, jotted notes on his clipboard, hovered over two glass-faced isolation chambers as Jones entered, drying himself with the towel. Both chambers, Jones saw, were connected to a refrigeration compressor which was running softly. One of the chambers was occupied by a chimpanzee, Julie, the other chamber empty. Digital thermometer readings clearly indicated identical temperature inside both chambers. Twenty-two degrees. Discarding his towel, Jones peered down at Julie wired to outside gauges monitoring respiration, heart rate, blood pressure and temperature. Though in a state of lethargy, the chimp appeared otherwise normal, no trauma.

Jones studied Julie's recordings, a long way himself from coming out of his lung-searing pain, none of which Enari noticed. He was in his element, had been working hard and loved it.

"I've been dropping temperature on a specified time course," he said. One degree every twelve minutes. Take a look."

Jones swallowed, fighting back a sudden urge to retch.

"You all right?" Enari asked with sudden awareness.

"This altitude. You think the next scoop of snow's going to be your last."

"Take some oxygen."

Enari started toward a tank, but Jones gestured him away from it, returned his attention to the chimp.

"He looks comfortable," Jones said.

"I've scanned him pretty thoroughly. No excitability."

"Enuresis, encopresis?"

Enari shook his head, no.

"We got a nice adaptable client," Enari said.

When Horner's voice was heard coming in over the short wave radio. Jones nodded, he'll get it.

In the kitchen-common room Geronimo was in a state of high agitation. He had accepted the couch as his world by now, but that was the extent of it. His distress, however, was over the short wave radio. He hated it, hooted and shrieked at it, showed his teeth in a display of outrage as once again Horner's voice was heard.

"Base to summit! Calling summit!"

Entering, Jones moved to the radio, flipped the two way transmission key, his presence partially settling Geronimo who quieted to hard thinking, eyes constantly gauging the radio.

"Five o'clock," Jones said, still heaving. "The bar is open."

Horner's voice, when he answered, was congenial.

"Listen," he said, "your data on the chill factor is really setting up."

"Okay," Jones answered.

"That's not very enthusiastic."

Jones shook his head, too exhausted for enthusiasm.

"We still don't know their tolerance range," he said.

"What's your projection?"

"We're taking one of the little fruits down to fifteen degrees."

Horner chuckled.

"You don't sound like you're making any new friends."

Jones glance at his bandaged finger.

"They're nothing to fool with. They'll take off a finger if you give them a chance."

"Are you still running tapes?"

"Running tapes on everything."

"It's working okay?"

"The recorder? Sure."

"I don't know why the hell we got nothing on Vogel's," Horner worried. "I mean, the damn thing doesn't just reverse and erase on its own."

"We talked about that. Best guess, he probably hit the reverse switch accidentally or to correct a notation but it was frozen. It activated when it thawed. Something screwed up."

"Any development with Geronimo?" Horner asked dismissing it.

Jones glanced at the chimp.

"We're letting him have the run of the place. He won't venture off the couch except to take food and water or use the sand box."

"Figures he'd be slow coming around. The altitude."

"It's not the altitude."

"What's that?" asked Horner, provoked.

"What's what?"

"You implied an inference."

"He's fearful."

"He would be. Brand new incompatible environment."

"It's not that kind of fear," Jones said. "He acts like there's an impending assault."

"Like what?"

Jones shook his head.

"Maybe I'm at two and two make five."

"We got the autopsy on Vogel, by the way," Horner said, switching topics. "It came in this morning, a little surprise. No heart attack."

The statement came in like that, no build to it. And it caught Jones unprepared.

"Hello summit," Horner's voice came over in answer to the sudden silence.

Jones looked up at Enari who stood in the entrance from the corridor. He, too, had heard the pronouncement. Jones stared back at the radio.

"No heart attack?"

"Blood enzymes and arteries clear, lungs clear, no vascular disorder. No clots or obstructions."

"What's the rest of it?" Jones asked. "Injuries?"

"No broken capillaries, bones or veins. No internal bleeding. It's a clear pathology. I'm afraid that window got him, he froze to death."

No one answered.

"Okay?" asked Horner.

"Talk to you tomorrow," Jones said.

"Good enough, summit" Horner answered.

"Summit out."

"And out."

Jones flipped the key, held there, staring. Enari gestured, simple surprise.

"Froze to death."

He moved into the room, past Jones who was still staring at the radio.

"Poor bastard," Enari said, shaking it off. "Damn."

Jones lifted his head, thoughts tumbling.

"I'd like to go over the food deprivation workup with you," Enari went on, dismissing the report on Vogel. "It's the next one programmed. I want to use two of the more aggressive pigtails…"

Jones mind was elsewhere, considering factors beyond understanding.

"Robert?"

"What?"

"Food deprivation. I want to use the pigtails."

Jones turned, stared at Enari. It seemed a shadow has fallen on Jones. But there was no shadow.

"Stay with the chimps," he said at length. "We'll use Geronimo."

"No. No," Enari objected. "I don't want to do that!"

Jones looked at him, eyebrows arched in surprise.

"What I mean," Enari said quickly, "the others are more seasoned, that's all."

"You're going to start some talk around here," Jones admonished facetiously.

"You can't stick him full of needles any more than I can," Enari pleaded. "Come on."

Jones held on Enari. He was looking through him.

"I'll meet you in a minute," Jones said. "Let me shut down that water."

In the generator room Jones shut down the stream of hot water playing down from the hot water tank onto the snow, now mostly melted. He held there a moment, immobilized. Within his brain some seismic disturbance was taking place, some revolution of thought he was powerless to resist. Quick images of Vogel played through his mind. He turned, moved into the corridor, looked toward the electronics room.

Drawn by an uncontrollable summons, Jones moved toward it, reached the open door, stared in. Nothing was changed from before. Tape recorder, bench table supporting anemometer, electronic calculator, swivel chair before the bench, storm window closed and locked, computers. His cursory survey completed, Jones looked down at the door opening in from the corridor. It was opened or closed by matching latches on either side of the door. It could be locked, he saw, could *only* be locked, by a dead bolt lock worked off a key and only a key, again on either side of the door. Reaching inside his pocket, Jones produced the ring of keys given him by Adams. As the keys to the monkeys cages, these too were labeled. Finding the proper key, Jones inserted it into the dead bolt, turned the key back and forth, found it worked well and properly.

Leaving the keys hanging from the dead bolt, Jones moved into the room. His eyes taking in everything, there was something about his face unseen before, something predatory, but calm. He circled about. Past the storm window. He looked toward the chair. Again a quick image of Vogel as found, a brief moment only but enough to reveal Jones' provocation. Vogel's face. It was that of a creature about to be struck, lips lifted and snarling, like a dog's, eyes gleaming with fear and helplessness.

Jones pulled back slowly. Something inside him was in revolt, perplexing, defying explanation.

It was later that night. Jones and Enari sat facing each other at the dinner table, the evening meal Enari had prepared before them. Mountain House Freeze-Dried Beef Stew.

'A delicious blend of tender beef with home-styled diced potatoes, carrots, sweet garden peas' the package promised.

Jones had scarcely touched his plate. Not Enari. There was an exultance about him as he ate, hurriedly, half chewing his food, washing unmasticated chunks down with coffee.

"All things take time," Enari was going on, "but I've got a surprise for you. We're getting organized. You look around you think you'll hear bugles, but we've had a break in the weather and Horner's all right, really. You can't expect him to grasp all issues, but he's beginning to understand you don't come up with answers in a day."

He rose with his plate, dropped off a morsel of food for Geronimo as he passed the couch, moved on to the stove.

"I eat too much," he continued. "I should try to cut down. It's not that there's any real physical harm in it. It's the psychological effect, too easy to gratify." He loaded his plate. "I'll probably cut down."

"It doesn't scan, Frank," Jones cut in.

"Oh, well, you know—you never know, do you."

"It doesn't scan."

He lifted his eyes, stared into Enari's earnest face.

"What's the trouble?" Enari asked.

Jones held on Enari, then lowered his eyes. His face, for the moment, appeared shadowy and insubstantial.

"Ever seen it before?" Jones asked.

"Seen what?"

"A man frozen to death."

Enari shook his head in confusion, no idea where Jones was going.

"There's a peacefulness comes over his face," Jones explained. "Muscles relax. Like going to sleep."

"I'm terrible at reading between the lines, Robert. What's going on?"

"Vogel looked like he was being bludgeoned to death. His eyes were wide, he was cringing in terror."

"What are you talking about?"

"I don't know," Jones admitted.

"What do you *mean*, you don't know."

"I don't *know* what I mean."

Enari laughed. He didn't know whether to take Jones seriously or not.

"You can't just ascribe an attitude to a dead man by what you think was on his face."

"Unprofessional."

"Damn right."

"Suppose he was actually in physical dread."

"Look—you've had a rough day, you called it yourself. You heard what Horner said, Nobel physiologists brought out, couldn't add two and two…"

"Yeah, but suppose."

"You can't make assumptions like that!"

"You bought Adams assumptions."

"Of course…"

"That Vogel *thought* he was locked in that room when he wasn't. That he opened the window, to what, escape, when he knew it would kill him? That's logical?"

"It was logical because there was nothing to contradict it!" Sweat was breaking out on Enari's brow. "He was psychotic! You said so yourself. You saw this place. He took it apart."

"He went to that room," Jones tried to puzzle it. "Why? It was the only room with a lock on the door, he could lock himself in. But he didn't, the door wasn't locked. He opened the window." He was repeating himself, struggling for answers. "Knowing it could kill him. Why? And the tape…"

"I don't find anything that can't be simply explained," Enari said. But the sweat beads were growing. "I think it's just what we thought. Vogel activated the recording control and it froze 'til it thawed…"

"But why the window, and that damn door. It doesn't add up, Frank. I don't think we know how Vogel died. I don't think we've got it right."

"I won't take your word for that, 'It doesn't add up'! What the hell are you up to, Robert?"

Jones thought for a moment, shrugged.

"Maybe…" He broke off, his thought incomplete. "I don't know, some little mistake in thinking. It'll turn up. I'll work it out in the shower."

He left, moved into the corridor, leaving Enari standing, feeling an inexplicable sense of disquiet.

In the upper bay that night, wide awake on his sagging mattress, Jones stared at the moonlight playing in through skylights. Not once had he closed his eyes. Two beds away Enari lay with his back to Jones, the rise and fall of his blankets coinciding with his breathing.

Jones, try as he willed himself, could not shake confoundment from his mind. He threw himself onto his side, listened to sounds. Enari's breathing. The constant hum of the generator. When suddenly—it came so subtly, Jones was scarcely certain— there was a premonition of something. An aura of things hostile, made manifest by messengers too refined for the senses to know. But an aura he felt and knew not how he felt it.

As subtly as it came it seemed to pass, Jones settling once again—when suddenly there were sounds, not of the mind, but audible hoots and screeches, quick and furtive.

Throwing back his blankets, Jones bolted upright to the edge of his bed. The sounds came from below, filled with mounting alarm.

Rising sharply, Jones, dressed in pajama bottoms only and barefoot, clumsily negotiated the semi-darkness, reached the stairs, moved down, came off them, no illumination in the corridor, quickly moved to the examination and housing room, looked inside. The room was lit by a night light. The monkeys were in a state of frenzy, something seemingly terrifying them.

Jones entered, his eyes passing quickly from cage to cage, the monkeys like hunted animals, pitiful and feverish, who knew the hunter had caught the scent and were powerless to escape.

Every force of Jones' being impelled him to spring up and confront the unseen danger. But what danger? Where? His eyes, searching the room, showed him nothing. Turning, he moved back into the corridor. Empty. Jones strained his ears. Not a stir. Only the monkeys in their distress. He fought to dominate panic. But his mind, considering every factor, showed only his helplessness. Suddenly, or was it his fancy, he caught sight of something. Sure enough, narrow as straw, extending from the top to the bottom of the doorway at the far end of the corridor, there was light. It was coming from the electronics room.

Jones held. How long he'd no idea. Silently he eased down the corridor, his bare feet padding on the cold cement floor. A quick puff of night wind caught the building. He shivered, though the wind hadn't touched him, continued gliding down the corridor, the light glowing through the crack in the door as Jones approached.

In an agony of fascination and anxiety, Jones reached the door to the room, stopped. Very gently he pressed his fingers against it. It yielded to his pressure, swung slightly open. Jones hesitated, then pushed the door all the way open, exposing the electronics room fully. The medical analyzer, he saw, had been turned on, was radiating light from several indicators. Crossing to it, Jones stared with incomprehension. There was nothing forbidding. All else in the room was the same as last seen. He cut off the analyzer, turned it on again to verify that it was working properly, again cut it off, leaving moonlight shafting in through the window.

Jones scanned the room, not at all sure what his next move should be. More puzzled than provoked, he slumped to the swivel chair, tried to analyze whether he'd just experienced an extraordinary event, or simply overreacted to a too fertile imagination. So preoccupied was he, he did not realize the room was cold, that his breath was steaming from his mouth. Crossing his legs, he massaged life back into one of his two chilled feet—all at once stopped. There was water on his hand. And on his feet. He looked down. Water covered the floor of the room. He looked about startled, suddenly was staring. The storm window was seeping water from melting snow.

Rising slowly, not quite believing what he was seeing, Jones crossed to the window. It was open. Three or four inches only, but open. But how? From what? Reaching it, he closed the window, secured the latch firmly, stood there, silent with incomprehension, wondering whether or not he was hallucinating—when suddenly there was a sound that chilled his heart. He whirled. The door to the corridor was creaking closed.

Galvanized, Jones leapt for the door, his fingers sliding in between the door and the jamb before it closed. Immediately he staggered back, flinging the door open wide, fell painfully against the corner of the table. For a moment he stood frozen, as though not daring to move. And yet there was nothing else for him to do. Breath labored, fighting fright, he pushed off the table, crossed to the open doorway.

In the corridor the distance between one end of the building to the other was a hundred feet, thirty-three yards. It looked like a thousand as Jones emerged from the electronics room, stood staring down. Nothing was in sight. The whole place could be deserted, so absolute was the silence, except for the hum of the generator. Not even the monkeys were heard any longer. Jones started up corridor, stopped, steeled himself forward again, retracing his steps. A pop of wind buffeted the building again, quickly abated as objects loomed before him, so familiar in daylight, now threatening. Trembling, yet with inner control, Jones, stopped to listen for sounds of pursuit, heard nothing, moved on, past recesses and doors. Regaining the examination and housing room, he looked inside.

The monkeys were settling back to rest. Whatever it was that upset them was gone. Allie alone was up and pacing. At the sight of the scientist, he stopped, stared through the wire meshing of his cage. Jones held on the monkey, trying to fathom events. He turned, moved out, leaving Allie to resume its pacing.

In the upper bay Jones came off the stairway, managed to stumble feebly to the edge of his bed and sat on it, fatigue immense. He called out with a soft, strained whisper.

"Frank?"

No answer. Enari's covers softly rose and fell on a man at rest. Almost before he could stretch his exhausted limbs upon it, Jones fell onto the top of his bed. Across from him Enari lay on his side, back to jones. His eyes were wide open.

DAY TWO

"I'M BEGINNING TO FEEL like Alice about to fall into the rabbit hole, stuffed into a tea pot, in a world as foreign as the Mad Hatter's."

They were in Fogel's office, Elinor and Aaron, the morning of the second day. She was standing at the barred window, staring out at the work-out area, watered down, for the moment empty.

"The normal is the schizophrenic," she went on, "who hears voices in his feces. Or the imposter who would have you believe it was God's will ordering him to eviscerate his wife. But *this* one."

"I didn't say it would be easy."

"You didn't say much of anything, Aaron."

"No. I didn't."

"He has the most bizarre stare I've ever seen," she said at length.

"They'll do that. You're the court."

"That's not it, it's not me."

"What then?"

"It's like he's trying to avoid understanding. But there's a powerful pull toward disclosure. Is he sedated at night?"

"He's refused."

"Any waking up screaming?"

"No."

"No undecipherable words?"

"No."

"Insults?"

"None."

"God knows he's bright enough."

"To know what he's done?"

"I don't know that he *does* know."

Aaron stared at her.

"You're serious."

"He's not what I expected, Aaron."

"Evasive, you suggested."

"About that, he was in the beginning. But I'll tell you. I think he wants answers as much as we do."

"You don't think he knows."

"What he's done? I don't know. That's his battleground and it's relentless. Denial vs discovery."

"Which is stronger."

"He's a scientist. He can't escape it. Exploration's in his DNA."

"Can you break him open?"

She thinks about that a moment.

"He's going to be destroyed, Aaron. Either way."

Enari sat at the table in the interrogation room, unmanacled, rubbing his wrists. Across from him sat Elinor with her file. They were alone.

"Good morning," she opened their meeting, a half smile on her face, purposely placed.

He made no effort to respond.

"All right," she answered, and referred to her notes. "Let's begin where you left off. You were aware Doctor Jones was awakened during the night…"

"Why do you bother. You won't understand a word of it," he said.

"Well, then help me."

"Why do you try so hard to be pleasant?"

"Is that what you're hearing?"

"Lovely, delicious," he answered sarcastically.

"Interesting choice of words. Not the sort I usually hear in these circumstances."

"What is it you want?"

"The truth."

He thought about that, settled on, "There's no such thing."

"Let's start with that."

"You look for trouble, don't you?"

"Only because I'm pretty sure of finding it."

"You go through everything. Dementia, psychosis, illusion…"

He broke off, shook his head, she saw, almost imperceptibly. Was he out of word play or was it despair?

"There's a question on the table, Doctor," she said. We have today and tomorrow. That's all."

He met her query with a look she sensed was about to bring on tears.

"What is it you don't want to remember?" she asked.

CAGES

AWAKENING IN HIS UPPER BAY bunk to a vague awareness of daylight, Jones listened to the swaying and creaking of the wind working through the outer recesses of the building. His eyes still closed, he savored the luxury of relief that followed a nightmarish night already blurring.

He opened his eyes. A brackish light poured in on him but not as he expected. With rapid adjustment of perceptions, he realized the window through which the morning light so usually entered was opaque and clouded with inner frost. Also steam was pouring from his mouth. At the same moment, his eyes lit upon his own uncovered body sprawled atop the blankets, and he perceived, with a sickening backlash of emotion, that there was no heat, that the room was freezing.

He bolted upright. Enari's bed, he saw, was empty. He bounded to his feet, pulled on pants and shirt as he slipped his bare feet into shoes, muffled an oath as he barked his shin against the bed frame, ran for the stairs, came off them at the same moment Enari, clothes thrown on, burst into the corridor from the shop, a can of fuel oil in his hand.

"Get the generator!" Enari shouted. "All the lights are out, there's no electricity!"

"*Gen*erator..!?

"I can't get it started!"

Bolting past Enari, Jones ran the length of the corridor, turned into the generator room. It was freezing cold as Jones entered, the generator turned off, inoperative. Moving quickly,

Jones grabbed the pull cord used to start the motor that powered the generator, yanked on the cord, once, twice. Nothing. He opened the choke, yanked back on the cord once more. Nothing. Turning fast to the water-making vat, Jones knocked off the cover, stared down at a sheet of ice covering the top of the water. He plunged his fist into it breaking the covering ice, opened the valve on the hot water tank. Only a trickle of water issued from the arching nozzle. Jones bolted back into the corridor, shouted to Enari.

"Open all the water taps!"

Enari was relighting a heater, looked up, startled.

"I've got to relight the heaters…!"

"No!" Jones answered furiously. "The water's freezing! It'll burst the pipes!"

He didn't wait for Enari's assent, headed back into the generator room as Enari turned quickly, moved into the examination and housing room, the monkeys thrashing about in their cages as Enari quickly crossed to the taps, opened them. A slim trickle of water came out.

In the generator room Jones pulled again at the pull cord. And again. And again. No response.

In the lavatory-shower room Enari threw open the taps on the sink to a thin trickle of water. He crossed to the taps on the shower. Another thin trickle.

In the generator room Jones closed the choke, pulled again on the cord. A cough from the engine. Another yank. Another cough.

In the kitchen-common room Enari entered at a run, moved past Geronimo who had fled to the top of the refrigerator, electricity out, motor dead, but the highest sanctuary in the room, the chimpanzee shivering and chattering as Enari reached the sink, turned on the taps. A thin trickled of water dribbled out.

In the generator room Jones was panting with exhaustion, face bloated from the exertion. His skin turned purple as he yanked on the cord. It failed once again. With the last of his strength and control, he hauled again on the pull cord. The motor caught weakly, Jones leaped for the fuel mixture control as it threatened to die—coughed—coughed—then mercifully began to purr.

In the kitchen-common room Enari spun about as the lights went on, the motor to the refrigerator once again on, too.

In the generator room the generator's motor had settled down to its proper hum. Turning fast to the water heater, Jones dropped to his elbows and knees, saw the electrically fed heating coils underneath the water heater were beginning to glow red. He pulled back exhausted, a look on his face of confoundment and trepidation.

In the kitchen-common room Enari poured coffee into a cup from a steaming kettle, set it back on the stove. He looked up at Geronimo. The chimp still squatted atop the refrigerator, still shivering, cowered from Enari's approach.

"It's okay, boy. Come on. Everything's okay."

Soothing as Enari's voice was, it was no solace to Geronimo, who shrank back against the wall. Turning, Enari looked toward Jones, collapsed at the dining table, hands cupped about his coffee.

"Well," Enari said, glancing at his watch as he set down his coffee. "It's nine. We'd better get on it. I've set up two isolation cages in the workup room for the food deprivation. We'll use Freddie and Napy. I'll have to transfer them under sedation, all this is turning them mean. I could use a hand."

Enari waited for a response, got none. He exited into the corridor leaving Jones alone, mid-room. Inside Jones thoughts tumbled, a ferment of wild stirrings he could neither control nor decipher. He looked at Geronimo, still cowering atop the refrigerator. He approached the animal, slowly. The chimp shrieked, bared its teeth. What had happened to it? From confused lethargy to terror. Why, what had caused it?

In the examination and housing room the monkeys watched in a state of hostility and apprehension as Enari, standing at the examination table, held a vial of ketamine, a short-acting anesthetic, drew several units into a disposal syringe. Withdrawing the needle, he lowered the vial as Jones appeared from the corridor.

"Freddie," Enari directed, a strained coolness in his voice.

Two pull bars protruded from either side of each cage. Jones crossed to the cage housing Freddie, a chimp. Instantly the animal set off a screech of protest, knowing full well what Jones' approach meant for him. Grabbing the two pull bars, Jones withdrew them. The back of the cage was brought forward, clamping the monkey firmly to the wire front of its cage. Immobilized, its haunch was an easy mark for Enari's needle.

"I'd like to know," Enari began, his voice forced and condescending, "maybe you can tell me—I mean what exactly…" He didn't know how to say it. "The next time you want to lower the heat in the middle of the night, use a light, a flashlight or something. Lower it, don't cut it off. That was close."

"I didn't get near the heater last night," Jones answered.

"It was an honest error," Enari said. "I'm not accusing." He withdrew the needle. "You didn't mean to do it. You made a mistake. It could have been critical, that's all I'm saying. Let's both watch it."

"Frank, I didn't get near the heater. Nor the generator."

Turning to the examination table, Enari discarded the used syringe, took up a second one, began filling it with ketamine.

"Robert, I saw you," Enari said. His tone was indulgent, forgiving. "You went downstairs."

"You *were* awake!" Jones answered, jumping on it. "You *heard* it! You *must* have heard it! Something was frightening the monkeys, Frank!"

" You know…"

"I couldn't see anything," Jones cut in. "The whole place was dark except for a light in the electronics room. Did you use the medical analyzer yesterday?"

"I haven't used it since we've been here," Enari said, controlling irritability, his second syringe filled.

"Neither have I. It was on," Jones said.

He had turned to Napy's cage, hauled back on the pull bars, clasping the pigtail virtually before it had a chance to protest.

"The window was open. The place was almost freezing. Water was melting in from the snow. I went over to close it. I closed it. The door to the corridor begin to swing shut."

"You opened the window, the draft closed the door."

"I'm going to open that window at two o'clock in the morning with the temperature outside at twenty below?" Then, appealing, "You don't see the pattern?"

"No, I don't see the pattern. What pattern?"

"To what happened to Vogel."

Enari drove the needle into the clamped pigtail.

"Honestly, Robert. You're so damn turned *on* about this thing, you've got nothing else to *do* with yourself."

"Frank, look at me."

"It could cost you our lives, messing around like that…"

Jones' hand shot out as Enari withdrew the needle, grabbed Enari's face, pulled it around to face his.

"It's not what happened!"

The utter conviction on Jones face brought a flicker of doubt to Enari's, a fleeting thing, like windflaws across the surface of a lake, when Horner's voice was heard down corridor coming over the short wave radio.orner's voice Horner's voice came over theshortwave down thecorridor.H

"Base Station to Summit Laboratory. Base to Summit. Come in."

Enari held, jaw clenched, stared at Jones. He turned from the room.

In the kitchen-common room Geronimo, still atop the refrigerator, hooted and hissed at the radio as Enari entered, flipped the two way transmission key.

"Summit Station," he said. There was a tightness in his voice and it was palpable.

"Read your barometer," Horner's voice came through.

"Good Lord, Horner! I've got two monkeys under sedation!"

"Read it, you'll see why. You've got snow coming in."

"Duly noted," Enari replied. "We'll bring in the laundry."

"Make sure your water supply's up to level. That's all I wanted to tell you. It's impossible out there when it's snowing." There was a pause. "What's wrong?"

Enari's eyes came up. Jones was standing in the entrance from the corridor.

"Enari?" Horner's voice was developing an edge of concern.

Both men, Jones and Enari, stared at each other.

"Let me talk to Jones," Horner said.

"No, it's…" Enari cut in quickly. "I'm not feeling too well…"

"There's something wrong, Enari," Horner cut in. "What is it?"

Again Enari hesitated.

"Enari?" Horner's voice was insistent.

"We lost our heat last night," Enari said at length.

"For God's sake..!"

"Somebody just forgot to fill the oil," said Enari. He looked at Jones. "That's what happened."

"Don't start that..!" Horner warned.

"I've got those monkeys, Horner," Enari said impatiently.

"Let me talk to Jones."

"All's okay we're squared away," Enari said quickly. "Summit out."

He flipped the key, disconnecting communication, stood motionless, shoulders bunched with tension. He turned, moved wordlessly past Jones into the corridor. For a long moment Jones held. He followed, found Enari in the examination and housing room, discarding the disposable needles as Jones reentered.

"I think it best if I do the workups hereafter, Robert," Enari said, a forced control in his voice. "Alone. You keep the place running, water and heat. I'll show you my findings, you can review them." And before Jones could reply, "Play pool, play detective while you're resting. Just don't bother me! Leave me alone!"

Without a backward glance, Enari left, leaving the sedated monkeys to Jones who made no effort to follow. Jones looked at the monkeys. Freddie and Napy, already beginning to suffer the influence of the ketamine, were starting to slaver, to lose control of their muscles. The others, chattering sympathy, were throwing themselves about their cages. Except Allie. The pigtail was assessing Jones with unguarded hostility. Jones held on the monkey, turned to the others. What set them off last night? What now? What *was* it?

In the upper bay Enari sat on his bunk. His heart, a great lump in his throat, was choking him. His blood was chilled and he felt the sweat of his shirt cold against his flesh. He tried to assess the nature of things. But he was not equipped for that. Give him a result, he could deal with it, determine its validity. But not the unknown. So why was it the thought came to him? He tried to drive it from his mind. He couldn't. His eyes went to the library at the far end of the bay. Willing himself to his feet, he crossed to it, stood before it. His hand went to the third row from the top and took down a book, its pages pristine new, seemingly never having been opened. A gift from someone, or a volume someone had brought for light reading but never had. "Bigfoot. Reality or Legend."

Dropping into a chair, Enari opened the book to its forward.

Also known as Sasquatch, the foreword began, *Bigfoot is the name given to a cryptid ape or homind-like creature witnesses claim inhabits forests and mountains, mainly of the Pacific Northwest of North America and the Sierra chain. Described in reported sightings as a large ape-like creature, in the range of 2-3 meters (6.6-9.8 ft) tall, it is thought to weigh in excess of 230 kilograms (500 pounds), and is covered in dark brown or dark reddish hair. Purported witnesses have described it with large eyes, a pronounced brow ridge, and a large, low-set forehead, the top of the head rounded and crested. The enormous footprints for which it is named have been described as great as 60 cm (24 inches) wide. Thus its name, though most scientists discount its existence and consider it a combination of folklore, misidentification , and hoax. Proponents, however, claim it to be a viable, living being, omnivorous and nocturnal.*

Enari slowly shrank back in the chair, stared off. Folklore, hoax. Of course. Stupid how could he have thought anything else. Except his head was throbbing. And there was nothing he could do to stop it.

In the kitchen-common room it was night. Outside, as Horner had warned, it was snowing, heavily. Enari sat at the dining table. His dinner was before him, but he'd barely touched it. Across from him he had neatly set Jones' place. But there was no Jones. The tape recorder squatted in the middle of the table. Heavy with weariness, Enari spoke into the mike as the tape rolled.

"February fourteenth. Evening radio transmission with Base confirms snow storm."

He flipped the stop button on the mike, thought what to say next. He flipped it on again. His voice, when he spoke, was forced.

"Food deprivation tests started in A.M...."

From above there was the sound of pool balls colliding. Enari looked up, not so much in irritation as regret. He was lonely, did not like to be alone. He lowered his head, returned the mike.

"Freddie and Napy, placed on quarter rations of food and water. Symbiotic relationship disrupted by mid-P.M. Mutual hostility accompanied by anger, aggression."

He flipped the stop button, looked down at Geronimo, hovering under the table, beside Enari's leg, the animal in a state of great insecurity. Squatting on its heels, it had come to accept Enari as its salvation. Eyes on Geronimo, Enari flipped on the mike again.

"Continuing dependency behavior in Geronimo since A.M., accompanied by bouts of panic..."

Again from above, the crack of pool balls colliding, followed by a long hollow roll, then a clatter as a ball fell on top of others already in a pocket. The sound, to Enari's surprise, seemed to fascinate Geronimo who reached toward the ceiling, trying to fathom the source of the sound. Enari sat a moment, watching the chimp. Shoulders sagging he shut off the mike. His heart was not in his work, nor in his food. Petting the chimp, two forlorn figures, Enari looked toward the ceiling, depressed and wanting to make amends.

He rose, moved to the stove. The chimp went with him, gluing himself to Enari. Grabbing a plate, Enari ladled food onto it, set it on a tray, along with coffee and silverware and a paper napkin. Crossing the room, he snapped off the light, moved into the corridor, leaving Geronimo balefully looking after him, the chimp wanting to follow, but unwilling to leave the protective confines of the kitchen-common room he knew.

Pausing at the physical workup room, Enari looked in. In two isolation cages, side by side, Freddie and Napy, separated by screening, were shrieking and snarling at each other. Turning back into the corridor, Enari crossed to the stairs leading up.

In the upper bay Jones was at the pool table as Enari came off the stairs, the tray of food in his hands.

"I brought you your dinner," Enari said, voice thick, trying to patch things up.

"Thanks."

Encouraged, Enari set the tray down on a corner of the pool table..

"How's it going?" he asked.

"Okay," said Jones. "What kind of day did you have?"

"Lot done," Enari welcomed the question, eagerly jumped back into the program. "The food deprivation's set up. They're ready to tear each other to shreds right now. I'm curious about the next stage. Submissiveness and sympathy lameness, probably."

Jones took a shot, sank it.

"Where'd you learn that?" Enari asked, trying for light conversation.

"Thinking."

"Sorry," Enari shook his head, not getting it.

"College. This was where I'd do my thinking. Any time I had a problem to sweat, I'd work it out playing pool."

The reference didn't escape Enari.

"Feel like talking?" Jones said.

"Play you a game?" Enari answered, trying to avoid it.

Jones set the cue against the table.

"I'd like to talk," he said.

"Of course," Enari nodded.

"Everything you've said about me, Frank, is true. I *don't* like this kind of work, you *know* I don't, I *do* get bored…"

"Robert, those were careless…"

"You *do* know me," Jones overrode him. "But I know *you.* You *don't* like the unknown, the unexplainable, you don't like dark alleys." He went on as Enari opened his mouth to protest. "Be as honest with me as I'm being with you. You could never work unless the concept was laid out for you. You said so, it's true. I'm the theorist, you're the practical scientist, pragmatic, functional. That's why we're a team."

A touch of hostility welled up in Enari's eyes.

"I don't know what makes you worry this bone…"

"I did not open that window, Frank. I did not turn off the heat, I did not turn off that generator."

"Who did?"

"Or what?"

"Robert..?"

"You know as well as I do for the moment…"

"Exactly," Enari said accusingly. "I know as well as you do. You've said it."

"Don't block me out on this! Not yet..!

"You come to me and spin a vague yarn about—and so forth," Enari cut in. "Then you state you don't know why. I'm perfectly ready and willing to accept any facts, prima facie, you want to lay out on the table…"

"That's what I've been getting at…"

"I know what you're doing…" Enari tried deflecting.

"You asked, you listen!" Jones countered. "Vogel found himself in that room. The window was open on Vogel, the window was open on me. The door was closed on Vogel, the door was closing on me…"

Enari's face had darkened. He seemed to draw himself together, preparing for action.

"I've been patient with you, honestly, Robert…"

"The day we got here the heat was turned off," Jones pushed on. "This morning, the heat was turned off…"

"Why don't you just call out, 'Halt! Who goes there? Advance and be recognized!'"

"There's something, Frank. Vogel knew there was something."

"Deranged perception, delusion—you're running a hundred and forty degrees..!"

"What was it he uncovered?"

"*Listen* to you! Excessive unreasonable evaluations as you long them to be, not as they are…"

"What is it we're uncovering, Frank, that doesn't want to *be* uncovered?"

Enari slammed his hand against the tray, flinging food across the room.

"I refuse to carry on this conversation one minute further! That is final!"

Ripping the blanket from his bed, he headed downstairs.

The kitchen-common room was dark as Enari stormed in, snapped on the overhead light, threw his blanket on the couch, crossed to the stove, ignited the gas, slammed the kettle atop the burner, turned to the cupboard, took down a box of cookies, ripped it open. He moved on to the desk, dropped into a chair, feeling suddenly weak and ill. Assuring himself that he was awake and in possession of his faculties, he turned to his clipboard, boldly lowered his eyes to lose himself in its contents—when all at once there was the sound of pool balls colliding above.

All was dark as Enari, fully clothed, huddled beneath his blanket on the couch in the kitchen-common room, tried for sleep that wouldn't come. Pushing back the blanket he sat up, stared starkly into the room. Guided by moonlight filtering in through the window, the storm now passed, he rose, crossed to the kitchen area, opened a utility drawer, took out a mini-flashlight, snapped it on, looked up at the ceiling, then about at his surroundings. Everything seemed quiet, serene. He moved into the corridor.

Coming off the stairway into the upper bay, silently, as to not awake a sleeping Jones, Enari crossed the bay to the library, hesitated, then played the flashlight over the titles 'til he found what he was looking for. "Bigfoot. Reality or Legend." He stared at it, almost, for the moment changed his mind. His hand came up, took it down. Lowering to a chair he snapped on the tensor lamp on the table beside him, opened the book. It wasn't a random search, he knew what he was looking for, soon found it, angled the book to pick up the light of the lamp.

One of the biggest mysteries in the world today is the tale of Bigfoot/Sasquatch, the seven foot ape-like-man-like creature reported to be inhabiting the upper reaches of the Cascade/Sierra Mountain Range of the Western United States as far back as the early eighteen hundreds. DNA hair samples, footprints and sightings, particularly in the past twenty-five years have produced a number of organizations that have developed with the goal of scientifically probing the existence of the biped.

Enari flipped pages to the following chapter, *Prominent Reported Sightings.*

1924: Prospector Albert Ostman claimed to have been abducted by Sasquatch... 1925: Fred Beck claimed that he and four other miners were attacked one night...

1941: Jeannie Chapman and her children said they escaped their home as a 7.5 foot tall...

1958: Bulldozer operator Jerry Crew took to a newspaper office a cast of an enormous footprint...

Enari read no more, he couldn't. He slowly raised his head. His face was malevolent—and stricken with dread.

END OF DAY TWO

IT WAS SEVEN O'CLOCK at night before Elinor left the hospital, made the two hour drive south to Goleta, just north of Santa Barbara, took the off ramp east to Cathedral Oaks, then left one mile, slowed, turned right through an unguarded entrance beneath an overhead sign which read, *El Batidor Ranch.* A hundred yards on an asphalt road, she turned left on a dirt one that climbed, headlights pushing back orchards of lemon and avocado groves. Reaching the top of a rise she turned up a driveway, circled onto a pebble covered parking area before a sprawling ranch house, security lights coming on, flooding the grounds as she braked to a stop beside a late model Mercedes.

Emerging from the car with her purse and papers, she was greeted by two dogs, tails wagging in recognition, one a shepherd, the other a rescue mix-breed.

"Hey guys!"

Giving each a quick rub, she turned, not toward the house but to an unlit path that led down to a forty foot trailer half hidden in a stand of oaks, wheels removed, resting on cinder blocks.. It was spring, and the only thing that gave her pause, especially at night, were rattlesnakes. The dogs had already tangled with one. Reaching the trailer, she pulled out her keys, unlocked the door and entered, snapped on the light.

The interior of the trailer was well appointed. Forward was the kitchen with refrigerator, cupboards, sink and stove. Mid-trailer was a table serviced by a semi-circular cushioned bench seat, several books in a rack behind. Aft was hot water heater, shower, toilet, bedroom. An overhead wire brought electricity from the house. Plumbing was attached, outflow deposited to a septic tank.

"Do not vacate your house." her divorce attorney had warned.. "Possession isn't nine tenths of the law, it *is* the law!"

The house referred to was a three bedroom Spanish style in Montecito, twenty-five miles south. Remaining in it was remaining in intimate proximity to her estranged husband who had refused to leave. She couldn't live with it. A classical pianist-lecturer of modest reputation she found one aspect of his reputation beyond modest. Playing and lecturing at universities throughout the country he carefully cast young female music students to turn the pages of scores as he played, successfully seducing more than his share in the process. He had come to the states from Belgium, swept Elinor off her feet, seduced her, married her, running through her money till he'd established himself. Mission accomplished, he now was on to higher social attachments, principally wealthy women who could further his career.

"My dear," Elinor was to hear him smugly say at their breakup, "there has not been a week of our marriage that I have been faithful to you."

Reclaiming her maiden name, it was while taking horseback riding lessons that Elinor met Orchid Fielder, an expert rider, owner of two Arabians, who counselled Elinor to abandon the son of a bitch, let the lawyers duke it out, offering at no cost the guest trailer she and her writer-actor husband, Millard, owned on their two acre property purchased outright from the El Batidor Estate.

Elinor hoped to never have to see her husband again. But that was not possible. She'd agreed to next Wednesday. Wednesday at the Santa Barbara Court House, a meeting called by their attorneys to bring a "civilized non-drawn out conclusion," as they called it, to the divorce. Or was it that the two lawyers had come to realize there was just not that much available for extended legal fees given the house was heavily mortgaged and the family's personal savings were all but drained.

Dropping her papers and purse on the table she turned to the refrigerator, looked over her options. She was exhausted, and the last thing she felt like was cooking dinner, well supplied though she was. Orchid had even made a casserole. Thank God for Orchid, and Millard. She settled on a bowl of corn flakes and a banana, brought them to the table, dropped to the bench seat, turned to her journal, fingering each page, reading none. No need. She'd memorized them all, and all validated her initial conclusions. Not in one was there a solution to her growing dilemma. Frank Enari was the least likely candidate for a criminal insanity plea she'd yet encountered. She'd felt that going in, assumed that. For all her expertise and experience, she was beholden to the one and only determination acceptable in a court of law. The M'Naghten Rule, defining criminal insanity for nearly two centuries.

'At the time of the committing of the act,' the rule stated, 'the party accused was laboring under such a defect of reason, from a disease of the mind…'

Defense attorneys habitually fought for it, asserting, she knew, 'an accused, in a criminal prosecution, avoids liability for the commission of a crime because at the time of the crime, the person did not appreciate the nature or quality of wrongfulness of the act.'

Never once had she heard of such a defense receiving a favorable determination.

'*From a disease of the mind!*' struck it down.

The rule specifically did not apply to momentary, transitory insanity. It accounted for insanity previous, throughout and after the act. But what of the act itself. What of the circumstances being so wretched, so stultifying as to create a moment of legitimate temporary dementia in an otherwise normal human being? Not allowed. Not acceptable by M'Naghten. Should it be? *Should* did not qualify with juries once prosecutors got through with them. That's what she was up against, had been brought aboard to determine. That the mind was diseased, not only during, but before and after to make a case and she knew it. And more than that, she realized, what had happened to her objectivity? What early conclusions was she drawing? With a shudder she shook them off. Stay professional, she counselled herself, stay on course.

DAY THREE

THE RANT CAME FROM a cell two down as Enari, lying on his cot in his own, could only listen.

"I am the victor instead of the killed. A fish, a fish, a fishy fish. Yeah that dude knew how to party, old school, baby. There've been way worse than him, he didn't kill that many people. Shove long-stem roses down his japs-eyes and jack off in front of the mirror. Used to cut holes in peoples' heads and pour acid on their brains so he could make his own sex slaves zombies. The worse part was the letter he wrote the girl's mother. Rape me I rape you back. Our father which art in heaven, so forth. Bad guys. So bad they got their own website. Searching the house, know what they found? Breasts used as cup holders. Human skullcaps used as soup bowls…"

When the sound of a key in his cell door brought Enari's attention to the door swinging open. It was Walter, cuffs and legs irons in hand.

"You're up."

In the interrogation room, Elinor was already seated with her folder as Enari was ushered in in chains.

"Good morning," she said with a smile.

Enari offered nothing in return as Elinor turned to Walter.

"Restraints off, please."

Clearly not comfortable with the order, but the routine established, Walter complied. When completed, Elinor nodded.

"Thank you," she said. It was clear he was to leave.

When the guard was gone, Elinor sat back in her chair.

"How was your night, Doctor?" she asked.

"You mean did they give me a sedative?"

"We can start with that."

"No."

"And?"

"'And' speaks for itself," he answered.

He was right. He looked worn, exhausted, eyes rimmed with red, jaw slacked, in need of a shave.

"Let's begin with something a little differently today," she said, opening her folder.

She removed several stapled pages.

"What is that?" His eyes were full on the papers.

"Just some tests."

"Tests. What kind of tests?"

"Well, let's start and I think you'll see."

She looked up at him. He sat back slowly as though awaiting a dagger.

"Just answer truthfully as it comes to your mind. So let's begin. Are you willingly taking this test?"

He stared at her.

"It's a yes or no."

He nodded.

"That's a 'yes' I take it."

"Yes."

"Do you consider yourself sane?"

It was a moment before he answered.

"Yes."

"Do you ever talk to plants?"

"Do I ever what?"

"Talk to plants?"

"No."

"Do you ever talk to animals?"

Again a moment.

"Doctor?"

"Yes."

"Do you ever talk to inanimate objects?"

"No."

"Do you ever talk to yourself?"

"Who doesn't."

"Have you ever had a meaningful conversation with any of the above?"

"Everyone talks to themselves sometimes."

"Yes or no."

"Meaningful? No."

"Do you hear voices in your head?"

"At times. Doesn't everyone?"

"If so, do you ever talk to the voices in your head?"

"Made up conversations?"

"If that's what it is."

"Sometimes."

"Do you often not understand what the voices are talking about?"

He stared at her, or through her, into himself.

"It's all right if you're not certain." She went on to the next. "Have you ever sought psychiatric help?"

"No."

"Do you enjoy setting fire to things."

"Of course not, no."

"Do you have an unreasonable fear of Aliens?"

"What?"

"An unreasonable fear of…"

"Why would I?"

"Are you an Alien?"

He laughed. "Some people probably think so," he said.

"Is that a yes?"

"No!"

"Do you sometimes have very violent urges."

"I guess like everyone."

"Do you refuse to believe things unless scientifically proved?"

"Yes." Emphatically stated. "Yes!"

"Do you have strong fear of something which you know does not pose any threat?"

No answer.

"Doctor?"

"No."

"Do you believe in killing off the weak to further evolution?"

"No!"

"Are you worried about the result of this test?"

"No. Why would I be? No."

"Are you purposefully lying to conceal your mental instability or stability?"

"What kind of question…"

"Yes or no."

"No!"

"Do you consider the person or persons closest to you as completely mad?"

"No."

"Have you ever?"

"No! Well…"

"What?"

"No."

"Do people not understand what you are talking about most of the time?"

"No."

"If this is so is it because you are many times more intelligent than they are?

"No!"

"Do you dislike the previous question?"

"Yes."

"Do you believe that most of the interesting conversations you have had are with computers ?"

"What's that prove, what's the point of this? There isn't an incisive question in the lot."

"Such as?"

"Do I stalk people? If I were an animal what would I be? End of the world, what would I do?"

"What would your answers to those three be?"

"No. Dog. Eat cheese."

"The purpose of the test, Doctor Enari, isn't to judge what you would say, it's to compare your answers to what others have said."

"My turn."

"I'm sorry?"

"The concept of conditioned behavior was popularized through the work of…"

"Pavlov."

"The concept of psychopathic personality…"

"Checkley."

"The Freudian concept of a death instinct…"

"Thanatos."

His shoulders drooped in despair.

"I'm not doing any more. I hate this."

"What happened after that night?"

"Brilliant. You actually had it working for a minute."

"You went to the library, took down that book."

He bounded to his feet, called off.

"*Guard!*"

"Tell me."

"True or false! Yes or no!" There was deep sarcasm and pain in his voice. "Encapsulating me in one word answers? With pre-determined questions, not even your own? That's your business? Well, look at yourself! Something you *witnessed,* experienced, heard, felt, tasted, saw, smelled? To go through *my* life? *You weren't there!*"

Elinor nodded her head in agreement, accepting his analysis.

"Take me there Frank," she said.

He fell back into his chair. She wasn't certain but she thought she saw his eyes well up with tears.

"I can't."

"You can do better than that."

"*I can't!*"

She regarded him a moment, then closed her notes.

"We're finished here."

She seemed about to rise.

"Pool balls."

"I beg your pardon?"

"He wouldn't stop. The pool balls."

BLACK ICE

A VIOLENT STREAM of water sprayed from a broken water line in the generator room as Enari, soaked to his skin, sweated out the pipe wrench, tightening a temporary clamp. The pipe tied off, the water leak stopped, Enari swallowed, exhausted, dropped the wrench to the concrete flooring, sat back a moment, retrieved the pipe wrench, trudged from the room.

Entering the shop room, Enari tossed the wrench on top of the work bench—stopped at the sound of colliding pool balls.

In the examination and housing room Enari was collating data. His head snapped up at the sound, the pool balls louder, echoing through the drum-like structure.

In the medical and research laboratory Enari had set up living quarters, brought down mattress, bedding and clothes. Seated at the work table, poring over blood samples and notes, he appeared wan and, for the first time, unshaven. The sound of pool balls colliding, louder yet, went through him like an electric Taser. He looked up, eyes raging at the ceiling.

In the medical and research laboratory it was night, Enari lying on his mattress on the floor, unable to sleep for the sound of footsteps pacing the upper bay above him. He fought for sleep.

His mind went to that girl in his class. She would come into his office, he fantasized, sit down on his couch across the room from his desk. She would be dressed in a short skirt, riding up her legs

"Anatomy and physiology," she'd say with what he knew was a manufactured entrance. "There's a connection between the two."

"Anatomy examines and describes the structure of living things," he'd explain. Her legs would by slightly parted, he'd see, allowing view between them, the pink of her panties. "It studies form while physiology looks at function," he'd continue.

"Anatomy looks at what is…"

"While physiology looks at what does."

She would nod. But he'd see through that. Her eyes would be on him, low-lidded, inviting, her breath would be shallow, breasts heaving.

"Can physiology be considered a sub division of biology?" she would ask, no effort to close her legs.

Throwing back the covers, Enari, dressed in sweat clothes, rose, went to the work bench, snapped on the desk lamp. Slipping into a chair, he addressed the gathering of voluminous notes he'd been compiling, had picked up pen to continue entries—when all at once the pacing stopped. Enari stopped too, waited for sounds he knew would follow. They came: the collision of pool balls. With an enraged sweep of his hand, Enari cleared the work bench surface of blood samples, beakers, test tubes, sent them splintering to the floor.

It was evening. In the kitchen-common room Enari was on the short wave radio. The kitchen, as well as Enari, had gone through a transformation. No longer was either well kept. Pots and pans lay about unwashed from meals a day or two old, condiments not put away. Enari's beard had several days growth to it now, his clothes were not clean, he needed a shower. He spoke into the mike, consulting a column of notes as Geronimo hovered close to his side. There was a marked testiness in Enari's voice.

"Displacement activities from thwarted drives."

There was a moment before Horner's voice responded after writing that down.

"Got that."

"Mechanisms for altering or controlling the general arousal level."

"Right."

"Mechanisms for modulating input from stressful stimuli."

"These all have a predictable temporal sequencing of actions?" Horner asked.

"You asked for cause of stereotypes."

"Of course, but…"

"If you want temporal sequencing, you ask for *that*! You do not ask for one thing and expect another!"

Silence.

"You asked for temporal sequencing, that's all," Enari said in more control.

Another moment's silence, broken by:

"Where's Jones?"

"Gracing us with one of his rare productive efforts. He's making water."

Another silence, followed by:

"What's going on up there, Frank?"

"That's all nonsense. I'll give you a temporal sequencing in the morning. Summit out."

He flipped the transmission key, sat down heavily on the couch, followed there by Geronimo. Instinctively Enari's hand went out to the chimp. There was the sound of Jones re-entering the building. Enari stiffened.

In the kitchen-common room Jones and Enari sat at the dining table across from each other, food before them. Except for the hum of the generator the place was silent, the two men silent, Jones nibbling at his food at best, lost in heavy thought, Enari not eating, keyed on Jones, and black from it.

"The butane needs changing on the generator," Enari broke the silence. It was not a reflection. He was launching an attack.

"The pressure's dropping on the stove and you might look through this while you're resting," Enari went on, shoving a sheaf of notes toward Jones. "Understand what's going *on* up here. And some doors to the monkey's cages need work. They're squeaking."

Still no answer. So preoccupied was Jones, he didn't seem to have heard. With a sudden burst of anger, Enari was up on his feet.

"I thought you were going to be sensible and drop this business!" Enari said.

Geronimo as always had followed Enari, who pulled away from the chimp.

"Coyotes survive at this altitude, Robert!" Enari plunged on. "Pronghorn sheep and some rodents! Eight orders of insects and three species of birds! That is all! The place is not being bombarded by ions, barometric phenomenon or cosmic forces! There is nothing unnatural here, or supernatural. There is you and me!"

Jones head came up. He stared at Enari. For all his plunging into thought and surmise he had come up with nothing.

"I want to know something," Jones said.

"Yes, you want to know…" There was acid in Enari's voice.

"Do you believe what you just said?" Jones asked.

Enari stared, with a look of slight disbelief. Was there self-doubt in that question?

"Do you really, in your heart and soul, believe all this is answerable?" Jones asked, "That nothing sinister happened to Vogel?"

Enari took hold of the opening eagerly.

"Robert…"

"You don't share my conviction? You don't share my concern? You haven't, not for a minute? I want to hear you say that, Frank."

"I can understand how you might have…"

"Say it, Frank!"

Enari was back into his chair.

"Robert, I don't even know what's been going through your head. The altitude. It's ludicrous. Just look around. If I was worried about anything here, I'm not an idiot, Robert, I'd go over the thing with you stem to stern, I'd tell you."

Jones held on Enari, tired, very tired, tired from digging snow and tired from alleys with dead endings. He lowered his eyes to the volume of notes that Enari had compiled. They blurred before him, but he tried to focus.

"Listen," Enari said, directing Jones to his report, "this is interesting. The action pattern of the monkeys doesn't always add up. I mean there're inconsistencies. You know the way bacteria will develop immunity to antibiotics? Well, sometimes these animals seem to have developed immunity to stress. They *appear* distressed, but I'm not sure." He's leafed open pages. "I ran laboratory tests on each workup, before and after…"

"Protein, enzymes, urine," Jones forced himself to concentrate.

"This is the food deprivation, for example," Enari went on. "The repeat workup…"

Jones flipped the pages forward and back.

"Where's the blood analysis?"

"I'm still on it. I'm doing a count in the lab," Enari said.

Jones looked up.

"That'll take days."

"I'll fill in the results. I've left space for it."

Jones stared at Enari.

"Since when are you wasting time on counts? That medical analyzer can run the whole assay in fifteen minutes."

Enari didn't look up. He avoided Jones' eyes, started to turn pages.

"I'm not certain yet about the correlation between body constitution and behavior, but…"

Jones' hand shot out, fell flat on top of the report, stopping Earni.

"Why haven't you used the analyzer, Frank?"

No answer.

"You haven't, have you? Not since we've been here. Because it's in that room where Vogel was killed."

"Died..!"

"You haven't set *foot* in that room since we've been here!" Jones drove on, anger building. "Have you? Why not? What could there be about that room that bothers you, Frank? You don't share my conviction. You don't share my concern. You'd tell me if you did." He angrily punched the report with his finger. "You've told me, Frank!"

For one dark moment Enari held his distress, the rage returned to his eyes. Pushing away, so hard he turned over his chair, he bolted from the room.

In the medical laboratory Enari was pacing. Moving with the un-witting care of a sleepwalker, he crossed and recrossed the room. There were no sounds from above. Jones, from all indications, was asleep. And sleep was what Enari craved, would trade his soul for. He couldn't. Fear and fantasy intruded upon his brain, and for all his intelligence, he couldn't reduce them. Suddenly, swiftly, he crossed the room to the corridor, moved into it.

As quickly as he entered, the corridor dimly lit by night-lights, Enari was filled with doubt. But doubt was no competitor for the naked, shameful agony he felt. With the furtive movement of a housebreaker, he closed on the door to the electronics room.

Reaching it, Enari stood in the open doorway to the dark-ened room, backlit by nightlights from the corridor. A long while he stood, unmoving, fearing to move. He entered. His breath in frightened little gasps, he made himself enter, past the calculators, past the window. His anxiety was hideous. But he forced himself to take in the place. He started, suddenly, at what he thought was a sound, careened, slammed back against the analyzer, held a moment in heart stopping terror! But there was nothing. Nothing! Not for all his quivering legs or panting breath or haunted eyes. The place was a room with electronic gear and a window that was closed and a desk and a chair. Unable to control them any longer, his legs gave out, he sank to his knees, head down, arms down, gasping paroxysms of relief when:

The shadow on the wall above him began to move so gradually at first, one would think it must have been the passing of the moon. Slowly it began to broaden, to oscillate, projecting on the wall the physical semblance of something alive, a creature beyond imagination.

A chill suddenly invaded Enari's body. He did not look up, but was shaking, stricken with the sense of vast impending threat. He dared not look around, but knew there was something behind and above him. His eyes grew wide with terror as the image on the wall writhed, a potency of motion. With a chocked cry, Enari whirled, arms lifted as though to ward off physical violence. He stared. Geronimo was shyly inching forward, through the doorway, arm extended in supplication.

In the upper bay Enari's bed was empty, its mattress removed, as Jones, alone in the bay, slept fitfully—when all at once there was a terrible clatter, a combination of sounds: the shattering pulse of machinery and a bestial cry filled with infinite protest and pain.

Jones eyes came open. Was he awakening from a nightmare, or entering one? The noise was no dream. He bolted from his bed. In undershorts only he ran for the stairs, moved down.

In the corridor below, Jones came off the stairs, the clamor louder. Lights everywhere were fully on. The first door to his right was the examination and housing room, fully illuminated. In their cages the monkeys thrashed angrily back and forth in full distress.

In the corridor Jones looked wildly about, saw light pouring out of the physical workup room. He ran to it. Inside, the treadmill was turned on, running at about three feet per second. On the treadmill, secured to it by harness straps, was Willie. Forced into quick, shambling, sore-footed steps, the primate screeched and hissed its pain and dismay to no benefit except for the tape recorder, turned on and recording its protest as Enari took notes. Jones entered, stared incredulous.

"It's three o'clock in the morning!"

"Notice something," Enari said. "Notice." He strived in vain to speak firmly, but his mouth was filled with saliva. "We may have analyzed something wrong."

Without breaking stride, Jones crossed to the treadmill, shut it down, slipped on handling gloves, undid the harness straps as Enari continued.

"Take that animal. Do you notice something? Compare this with what we did. For example, we demonstrate the fear hypothesis…"

The harness unstrapped, Jones picked up the badly shaken monkey, moved into the corridor, Enari following with:

"The fear stimuli produces a radical physiological change. Rage, hyperventilation, accelerated pressure and pulse…"

Reaching the examination and housing room, Jones entered with Willie, Enari entering also, continuing.

"Extreme fear abolishes or interferes with normal pain reflexes. Maybe we didn't have an adaptation at all the other day…"

Reaching Willie's cage, Jones opened it, the cage door squeaking audibly, the monkeys howling a mournful symphony for their fellow as he was returned to his cage, hating the two men with bitter eyes. Jones turned. Enari's legs and hands were trembling. Ghastly-faced, his chest rose and fell. The hostility on Enari's face as he looked at Jones, matched the monkeys. He took a breath. His voice, when he spoke, was more than accusatory. There was more than fear on his face.

"Do you really want the truth? Listen, Robert, I'll tell you, and no bull. The truth is you're pulling all this."

Jones closed and locked Willie's cage, moved past Enari out into the corridor. Unstrung, Enari fought to gather himself, moved after.

In the physical workup room the tape recorder was still turning slowly, still recording as Jones entered. Enari moved into the doorway behind him.

"I understand. I understand," Enari said, his face full of pleading. "You've got your own particular way of going about things, setting up your own situation. Just let me in on it, let me help you with it. I can make a contribution."

Jones lifted his head, soberly aware of his partner's fear, the fatigued brain, the edge of panic. He snapped off the tape recorder, held a moment, back to Enari, turned slowly, manufactured a smile that seemed to yield.

"We'll talk about it. In the morning," he said.

He planted a reassuring hand on Enari's shoulder, turned off the light, moved into the corridor, headed toward the stairs, snapping off corridor lights as he went. For a long moment Enari lingered trying to fathom his partner's sudden change of heart. Capitulation? Acquiescence to logic? Was it over, finally, all the nonsense? Enari for the first time in days felt life turning back to where it should be.

In the examination and housing room Willie, just now beginning to overcome the exhaustion and abuse of the treadmill, lunged with a burst of anger at the front of his cage. Nostrils distended, hair bristling, his jaws spasmodically wrench apart. A defiant, deep-throated vibration issued forth.

"Physiology aims to understand the mechanisms of living," he was explaining, "how living things work. Human physiology studies how our own cells, molecules and organs…" Enari was explaining.

"You're really very sweet, you know that?" the girl said from the couch.

His heart was beating so wildly he thought it would break through his chest.

"I don't know how to answer that," he said.

She answered it for him. She sat a moment, as though determining something, rose, crossed his office to the door, locked it, stood with her back to him, then turned. Her face held an expression he'd never seen before. It was flushed and filled with desire. And then she was moving to him, bending to him as he sat in his chair behind his office desk, his hands rigidly clutching the arm rests, and her hands were on his face and she was kissing him, soft lips, so soft, soft as he had never known. He could feel the growth in his groin, yet dared not move. She did that for him, extended a hand, took his, helped him from his chair, led him to the couch.

He didn't resist, he couldn't, even as she lowered them both to the couch. Crossing her arms before her, her hands reached for the hem of her sweater, pulled it up and over her head. She wore no brassiere, he saw, and her breasts, oh, God, so firm and youthful. And then she was slipping out of her shoes and undoing her skirt and lowering it to the floor. And then—oh, God, and then—her panties followed.

"You're shaking," she said.

"Yes." It was almost a whimper/

"Just close your eyes. There's nobody else, just us. Do you want me?"

She kissed him lightly and he responded, aware she was undoing his belt and lowering his zipper and pushing his pants and underwear down to his thighs and his erection was more than he had ever known. She fell back on the couch and her legs spread open and he went to mount her, when—No! Oh, no, not yet! *Not yet!* No *no!*

He bolted upright in his bunk, the fantasy dream gone with the ejaculation.

It took a moment to recall where he was, in the Quonset hut's upper bay, day broken cold and grey, exceedingly cold, with a subtle gloom, the beginnings of an icy snow crackling off the skylights, Jones in his bed, Enari occupying one of the others, his former bunk still stripped of its mattress. Jones stirred, pushed himself to an elbow, saw Enari rigid and upright.

"You all right," Jones asked?.

The inside of Enari's sweat pants were soaked, his labored breath slowly receding.

"Yes."

Jones nodded toward the skylights.

"Last sled for Dawson," he said.

"I know," Enari answered groggily. "I mean, I understand that. I see your point."

He threw back the covers, trying to shake off deep, almost drugged memories of his dream now quickly fading. He looked at Jones, a baleful look.

"Listen," he said,

"Last night, I know," Jones said, dismissing it.

"What exactly did I say?" asked Enari.

"Some talk about the adiabatic lapse rate."

"Funny."

"When's breakfast?"

"When do you want it?" Enari answered gratefully.

"I'm usually free about his time."

In the corridor below, Jones and Enari were moving off the stairs, Jones dressed fully, Enari still wearing his night sweats, carrying shirt, pants, socks, shoes as he turned in at the lavatory-shower room.

"Put the kettle on, will you? I'm going to grab a fast one." He pushed inside as Jones moved on.

In the lavatory-shower room Enari dropped his shoes and socks to the floor, threw his shirt over a towel rack, moved, sweat pants still on, to the shower stall, turned on the hot water tap. No water. He stared, bewildered, opened it wider. No water. He opened the cold water tap. No water. Turning to the wash basin he opened both taps simultaneously. No water. He pulled back slowly, stunned, turned sharply toward the door.

In the corridor Enari, barefoot, broke into a run.

"Robert! Robert, for God's sake, there's no damn water…!"

Reaching the kitchen-common room entrance, Enari stopped, stared in in disbelief. The food store, virtually all of it, food and condiments, were shredded and slammed about as though hit by a cyclone. Rice, flour, sugar, meal had been reduced to paste intermingled with broken glass jars of preserved fruit, syrup, juice and powdered milk. The door to the refrigerator was open, all contents swept to the floor and smashed. The freezer door stood open, meats and frozen supplies spilled out and defrosting. Kneeling on the floor, surveying the carnage, in shock, was Jones.

In the doorway Enari stood, barefoot, still in his sweat pants. He entered the room, avoiding the broken glass on the floor. His emotions, forever forced into fluctuation, never, seemingly, permitted to settle, could not cope rationally. His throat, naked and knotty, swelled with deep, uncontrollable rage.

"Damn your soul to hell!" he cried. "Hell's too good for you! I *knew* it was you! I guessed! I *guessed*! Get out the cigars and whiskey! We're not running a lab up here, we're running a hustle! 'Scientist Discovers Abominable Snowman At High Altitude Research Center,' that's the con, isn't it?"

Jones stared at Enari, at the face so positively fiendish, fists clenched and unclenching as Enari raged on.

"You fraud, you fake! The *genius* who's never arrived! You're not a man to be trusted, you never have been! Selfish, no morals! If you think you're going to buy yourself some kind of immortality with this kind of—why is it you haven't done great things in this world, Robert? You don't lack ambition, feeding off other people's talents. That's why you have it in for me! I'm your meal ticket! Always have been! Well, I'm a better man that you are! You're without nobility, Robert, you're a pauper..!"

When all at once Enari's rant froze mid-sentence. From above, a thunderous sound, something hard caroming off the floor, smashing against the walls! Enari stared at Jones, an utterly stupid expression on Enari's face. And the sound! Pushing off the floor, Jones bolted for the corridor.

Rounding the corner of the entrance to the room, Jones almost stumbled, held his feet, ran down corridor, took the stairs to the upper bay three at a time. Reaching the bay, Jones virtually plunged into the room, stopped, drew back. Behind him Enari, barefoot, came off the stairway, his breath caught up in a gasp as he stared with Jones in astonishment. Atop the pool table Geronimo was furiously bombarding the place with pool balls.

In the examination and housing room the door closed on the protesting Geronimo, safely ensconced in an empty cage alongside the others. Placing the padlock in place, snapping it closed, Jones placed Geronimo's name tape on its food box, held a beat, utterly livid, turned, moved wordlessly toward the door, past Enari, devastated with guilt, wishing for all the world he could find a hole to crawl in.

"It was my idea, my fault," Enari said, "We never should have let him run. He must have been angry because I wouldn't..."

Jones had not stayed to listen. Enari stood a moment, his heart going out to Geronimo, cowering in his cage. He turned into the corridor.

In the entrance foyer, at the far end of the corridor, Jones was pulling on boots. Reaching for his great cold-weather coat, he slipped it on, zippered the front, buttoned the over flap and the collar, pulled the hood down over his head, buttoned the under flap. Taking gloves from his pocket, he pulled them on, slipped his boots into snowshoes, grabbed the shovel, pulled back the bolt that locked the door, lifted the latch, stepped into bitter, driving snow, Enari moving into the foyer, mouth opening to speak, words that were never spoken as the door was slammed closed behind Jones.

Enari's shoulders sagged. Drearily he turned, crossed into the kitchen-common room, viewed the devastation. A sudden physical nausea wracked his body. Sick at heart, he slumped into a chair.

The frozen moisture of his breathing settled on his collar, lining it in a fine powder as Jones shoveled snow in through the storm flap. His beard and developing moustache was likewise frosted, taking the form of ice and increasing with every misty breath he exhaled, which came in short gasping efforts. He had been shoveling sporadically, unable to stand more than a few minutes at a time in the terrible cold. Therefore he had worked slowly, carefully, keenly aware of the danger of over-exertion and exposure. He had gone as far as he was able, half dropping, half driving the blade of the shovel into the snow, and now he was done. He made his way back around the corner of the building, stepping clumsily, gingerly, even with snowshoes, testing each footing for each step. Reaching the entrance he lifted the latch, shoved open the door, stumbled in.

In the entrance foyer Jones closed the door behind him, set the shovel against the wall, yanked open the under flap strapped to his throat. Caked with ice it was almost choking him. His head thrown back, he gasped, huge gulps of warm air. Kicking off his snowshoes he moved from the foyer into the corridor, struggled down it to the generator room.

Moving inside it Jones crossed to the water-melting vat, looked inside. The vat was about two feet from being filled. Turning on the stream of hot water, Jones moved to the storage tanks, check the level gauge. The tanks were about four-fifths full. He turned, trudged out, rubbing his cheekbones and nose with the back of his mittened hand.

In the kitchen-common room Enari had cleaned up much of the mess, was cleaning up more. The food that was salvageable had been restored to shelves, refrigerator and freezer. Soup simmered on the stove; there was food in the oven. Two emotions worked strongly on Enari: relief and guilt, and they surfaced varyingly as Jones straggled in, blue with cold and exhaustion, pulling mittens off with his teeth.

"Take your shower, if you want," Jones said angrily.

"Look—look, I don't need…"

"Take the damn thing, just take it!"

It was an order, and a hard one, and Jones' tone was filled with punishment. He unbuttoned his jacket. Rather, tried to. His fingers were numb. He crossed to the soup, reached for it. Enari sprang to be of service.

"Don't put that in a tin," Enari warned, "it'll burn your mouth. Here, use a plastic cup." He poured. "I'll have dinner in half an hour. I was able to save most of the food. He really shredded it."

He handed the cup to Jones who could not bring his fingers together to hold the cup, but was able to gather it between the palms of his hands.

"Do you have to go back out?" Enari asked.

"Yeah, once more."

"You've been in and out all day."

"Then *you* go!"

Enari flinched.

"I didn't mean—honestly…"

"It's twenty below. You can't last more than fifteen minutes at a time out there!"

"I see your point," Enari said. "I see what you mean."

Jones reflected on his own attitude. There was no future in it, no dividend. He sipped his soup, nodded satisfaction.

"Look," Enari began, "let me talk to you."

"Go ahead."

"Robert, I'm sorry."

Jones gestured it was over.

"No, no, listen, let me say it." Enari was almost pleading. "I got hot and frightened—all that stuff you were coming up with."

Then quickly, anticipating Jones' defense, "It's interesting. It *was* justified. It had me going, that's all. I got to admit that, it *sounded* like there was something to it. Put yourself in my position. I mean, God, you know, if you're a man who has—it bothered me. But I can see the point. The more I thought about it. It's hard to answer how A and B equals C.

Jones held for a moment, settled heavily into a chair.

"Hell, I don't know," he said.

"No," Enari answered, bending over backward to be supportive. "There is that business with Vogel…"

"Maybe Adams was right…"

"No, that door and the window have not been satisfactorily explained yet, Robert. We'll talk about it, we'll find it. It's there, a logical explanation, it's there."

"Something to do with that name," Jones said in reflection.

"Name? What name?"

"You and I were there, with Horner. We heard it together. Something about Vogel having a conversation with Alexander The Great."

"I don't know," Enari said, "What about it?"

Jones for the life of him couldn't put it together. He shook his head, rose.

"Whatever the hell," he said. "Turn off the water down there, will you?"

"You okay?" Enari asked with seemingly genuine concern. "You really okay?"

Things back to normal, Jones smiled.

"Go take your shower."

In the lavatory-shower room steaming hot water streamed down on Enari, bathing him in a luxurious sense of security and well-being.

Outside Jones worked with pain and lung-searing labor shoveling snow through the storm flap into the vat in the generator room. Fog now joined the blizzard, all but blinding and getting worse. Automatically, now and again, he changed hands with the shovel. But that did not help his cheekbones and nose. His moist breath quickly powdered his eyebrows, lashes and beard. There was no mistake about it. It was hideous cold.

In the shower, Enari lingered a moment longer. Water was at a premium and had to be rationed. Still he was loathe to give up the drowse that seemed the most comfortable and soothing he had ever known. But he must. He knew he must. Reluctantly he turned off the shower, stood there in tingling rapture.

Outside Jones struck his fingers sharp smashes against his leg to restore circulation, lifted the shovel of snow to the storm flap.

In the entrance foyer the bolt on the door latch was suddenly, no warning, driven solidly home, locking the door to all outside.

In the lavatory-shower room Enari had dried himself, had partially dressed, put on his pants and shoes. Slipping into his shirt as he exited, he moved into the corridor. Almost at the moment he entered, he was aware of it: a sudden premonition of danger. It seemed a shadow had fallen upon him. But there was no shadow. He tried to locate the source of the force, tried to sense the imperative presence. Only then did he become aware: there were sounds from the examination and housing room.

Irresolute, unwilling to encounter what he might find, he hesitated. But his feet were taking him down the corridor. Reaching the room, he looked inside. The monkeys were in a state of frenzy. Flashing forms of grey, with gleaming eyes and lolling tongues, they thrashed back and forth in their cages. One cage was open and empty. Geronimo's!

In the corridor Enari pulled back from the room, looked wildly about. His eyes went to the physical workup room. He ran to it, threw open the door. It was as last seen the night before. Freddie and Richie still occupied their isolation cages, but had entered a stage of withdrawal. Across the room snow and fog pressed densely against the windows, giving the daylight a dim tarnished quality. There was no Geronimo.

Outside in the snow Jones stamped his snowshoes, thrashed his arms, lifted the shovel for a close to last offering to the storm flap.

In the corridor Enari had run to the shop, looked in. Empty.

Outside the hut Jones drove the shovel into the snow once again—all at once stopped. His head came up. His eyes blinked with incredulity. He shouted with realization and dread as it hit him.

"*Alexander!*"

In the corridor Enari's sense of nightmare was deepening as he reached the kitchen and common room, looked in. It was as last seen, no sign of Geronimo.

Outside in the snow Jones rounded the corner of the building. Snow bit his face, the going was slow, each step a caution in itself. But he hurried.

Inside the hut Enari's movements had become frantic. He looked back. One room had been bypassed. The medical research laboratory. Reaching it he looked in. The room revealed nothing. He started to pull away, stopped. Some reflex signaled his brain. He turned, looked back. With stiff precision he entered, moved toward the work bench. Upon the bench various paraphernalia were laid out: test tubes, beakers, burners, bottles and vials of compounds. A narrow stream of blood was spilling onto the table, flowing over its edge, down onto the floor.

Every instinct and fiber of Enari's being favored flight. But flight to where? He stood, immobilized, assailed by fear. His eyes came up to the cabinet above the bench. He paused, irresolute, unwilling to encounter what he knew now to be the worst horror of all. With a quick movement, he pulled open the cabinet door—recoiled as Geronimo plunged heavily, face down onto the floor, mutilated, dead.

Outside, Jones had reached the Quonset hut entrance, lifted the latch. The door was locked closed, the latch holding fast. Jones lifted the latch again—and again—threw his weight against the door. It wouldn't budge.

"Frank!" he shouted. And again, "Frank!"

In the medical research laboratory Enari stood there, filled with awareness, the dead animal at his feet. He could hear Jones' desperate cry.

"*Frank?*"

Enari made no effort to move.

Outside Jones threw his shoulder again and again against the door. Again and again the bolt held. With the shock of realization Jones gave up. It was useless. A sudden fear of death, dull and oppressive, came to him—a fear that quickly became poignant as he realized it was no fanciful speculation. He drove the thought from his mind, flung a look about. Even without looking, he knew there was no window unlocked, no other door. He had only one hope and he headed for it, back toward the side of the building from which he'd come.

He was angry, and cursed his luck aloud. Because of that he plunged on with his snowshoes, lifting, slamming them into the snow instead of walking. He stumbled, tottered, crumpled and fell. When he tried to rise, he fell again. He must sit and rest. But even as he contemplated this he knew it was suicide to do so. He rose, moved steadily on now, with a careful, measured pace.

His beard was totally whitened by his crystalized breath. And he travelled more by instinct than sight, so dense was the driving snow and the fog. But he'd reached the corner of the building, rounded it.

And then it happened. At a place where there was no indication, where the soft unbroken snow seemed to advertise solidity beneath, he started to cry in panic as the ground gave underneath him. It was not deep. He went down only to his knees. But the snowshoes acted like toggle bolts, making it impossible to extricate them.

Lifting his boots free, leaving the snowshoes behind, Jones was reduced to crawling, to moving flattened on his belly. The considerable pit that he'd dug from shoveling snow offered a downward plunge as he reached it, brought him flat against the side of the building.

His hands now, so cold, were of little use to him in helping him back to his feet. He could trust only his legs. Because of their intense activity, circulation flowed through him sufficiently, and they responded, brought him to an upright position. Before him, chest high was the storm flap. He pushed his arms through then his head.

In the generator room Jones pulled himself through the storm flap. The huge vat, filled with half-melted snow, was directly before him. He opted for the rim of the vat, tried to avoid the freezing slush, only partially succeeded, one leg dragged in, falling into the vat. With all the energy at his command, he pulled himself out and over, tumbled cruelly down onto the concrete floor.

Panting with exhaustion, the ghostly snow mask on his face already beginning to melt, Jones worked at freeing himself of his coat. But he had no feeling in his fingers and hands to manage it. He came to his knees, tried to rise, his legs failing him once, then trying again, succeeding, stood there, gasping, trembling, holding onto to the rim of the snow-melting vat. His hoarse, croaking wheeze seemed to defile the immaculate hum of the generator. All else was quiet. He tried to call out.

"Frank..?"

His head ached unbearably. His throat was dry, offered little more than a croak. But he was conscious and more alert than he had a right to be. He called out again.

"Frank…?"

Still throaty and hoarse. Struggling to control his muscles, he ventured from the room, out into the corridor, stumbled, weaved, supported himself from falling, hands on the corridor's walls, called out once again.

"Frank!"

Voice firmer. Slightly. He reached the door to the lavatory and shower room. It's door stood open, no one inside. At the shop room he cast a quick desperate glance inside, saw no one, moved on, up corridor, reached the medical research laboratory, looked in, paled at what he saw.

Lying atop the work table was Geronimo. Or what remained of Geronimo. It had been no kindly death. It had been savage and vengeful. Jones moved toward the chimp.

A look came into his face of utter tragedy and distress. His hand went out to the animal, when Jones saw Enari. More real than the man was Adams' gun in his hand. Enari's voice, when he spoke, was almost as much of a croak as Jones', his face distorted with dementia, born of fear and helplessness. Enari made a supreme effort to collect himself.

"I'm not going to use this, Robert. Respect that, please."

"Frank, Frank," Jones shook his head.

"I'm just going to ask you simply, I want you to go into that electronics room. I'm going to lock you inside and radio Horner."

"You really think I did this?" Jones asked. "You know I didn't."

"I'll bring down your bedding. You're not feeling well."

"I didn't lock myself out, Frank. Did you lock me out?"

"Just go inside there, Robert, please…"

"You *know* you didn't. Who did? Geronimo? Not Geronimo."

"There's nothing to talk about, Robert…"

"There's a lot to talk about…"

"We've talked so very much…"

"You really don't know what's happening here, Frank?"

Enari glanced toward the electronics room.

"Don't turn your head away," Jones came on hard, "for once in your life! Look at it! *Look* at it! Food is removed from the monkeys, food is removed from us..!"

"It's no good, Robert..!"

"Subject the monkeys to panic and fear? We're subjected to panic and fear…!"

"It's been you," Enari cried, increasingly unnerved, "all of it you…!"

"Subject the monkeys to isolation, we're subjected to isolation…!"

"You've done all the damage you're going to do! It's some mental illness…!"

"Subject the monkeys to cold, we're subjected to cold," Jones drove on. "How far do I have to spell it *out* for you..?"

"I'm not going to let you walk over me, Robert…!"

"Everything that's happening here it happened before, to Vogel! *Look* at this place!"

"You're demented and dangerous, wanton destruction…!"

"Look at *you*, Frank! You're becoming Vogel, being made to become him! Subject the monkeys to pain, we're subjected to pain!"

Enari backed away, weak and trembling.

"I don't feel well, Robert, please…"

"Subject the monkeys to experiment, we're subjected to experiment. Don't you see it? Frank, it's the monkeys! Everything we've done to them, they've done to us!"

"No! How…?"

"Vogel told us what it was, and nobody heard him! Alexander the Great! He had conversations with Alexander! The monkeys, Frank. They were named after conquerors! Napy, Genghi, Julie, *Allie*…!

There was a crashing sound. At the same instant Jones received a shattering blow on the left side of his chest, and from the point of impact experienced a rush of flame through his flesh. In the next instant Enari felt Jones' grip at his waist. Then the grip broke free and Jones fell lifeless to the floor.

For a long moment Enari stood not knowing what to do, scarcely knowing what had happened. With a sudden passion of regret, he fell to his knees, started to unbutton Jones' flannel shirt, but blood was already oozing form the wound. Appalled, Enari pulled back. When suddenly through a haze of tears:

"We may have analyzed wrong, Frank. Take that animal. Do you notice something? Compare this with what we did. For example, we demonstrate the fear hypothesis…"

Jones' voice. But from where? The turmoil of Enari's imagination?

"The fear stimuli produces physiological change," Jones voice was going on. "Hyperventilation, accelerated pressure and pulse..."

Enari climbed to his feet. It *was* Jones' voice. He was actually hearing it. But from *where*?

"Extreme fear abolishes or interferes with normal pain reflexes. Maybe we didn't have an adaption at all the other day..."

Moving into the corridor Enari stopped.

"Maybe what we had was hypoesthesia, decreased sensitivity to tactical stimuli, producing, perhaps, partial tonic mobility..."

Jones' voice, Enari suddenly realized, was coming from the electronics room, He edged toward it, gun in hand, stopped short in the doorway. Inside the room the tape recorder sat on the desk, plugged in, tape rolling.

"Do you really want the truth? Listen, Robert," Enari heard his voice in protest. "I'll tell you, and no bull. The truth is you're pulling all this."

Enari moved into the room, drawn to the recorder as a moth to a flame.

"I understand. I understand, Robert," Enari's voice was going on. "You've got your own particular way of going about things, setting up your own situation. Just let me in on it, let me help you with it. I can make a contribution."

Reaching down Enari cut off the recorder, pulled his hand away as though from a hot stove, stood staring at it. Suddenly, inspired by a bitter waft of cold, he lifted his eyes and stared. The window was ajar, snow failing through the opening onto the floor. Incredulous, he backed away, turned fast toward the door, stopped cold. Napy and Gengi stood in the corridor, just outside the housing and examination room. Julie joined them. Then Freddie. And Willie. Their eyes blazed.

Enari wouldn't, couldn't believe it. He spun back into the room, turned again to the door and recoiled. In the doorway Allie, lean and hungry with bitter eyes was closing the door.

"Base to Summit. Base to Summit. Summit, Summit, come in."

In the Owens Valley Tower Mountain operations center Ryan Horner hunched over the short wave radio, dialed the volume to maximum. Static. Nor had there been anything other for the past twenty-four hours. No answer to calls. Shoulders rigid, Horner sat back, looked up at Val Adams in shared apprehension, rose from his chair, grabbed his cold weather coat from the rack.

The storm abated, skies cleared, the helicopter sat on its pontoons where it had landed just off the Summit Laboratory. In the chopper, the overhead rotors wound to a stop, Adams and Horner stared through the Plexiglas bubble at the entrance, dreary, desolate, the building half-buried in a new fallen sea of white. No word was spoken. Another minute passed. Two. It was Horner who made the first move. Pulling the hood over his head, securing his gloves, he threw open the passenger-side door, dropped to the snow. Adams following, Horner led the way, high-stepping, plowing, sinking, retrieving, through to the entrance. Reaching it, Adams close behind, Horner, to his surprise, found the door unlocked. He lifted the latch, pushed it open.

Emerging from the vestibule as he pulled off his gloves,, Horner drew to a stop, his knees almost buckling at the sight before him.

Littering the corridor floor, from the entrance to the electronics room, were the monkeys, all six of them, blood pouring from separate bullet holes in their chests or heads. None stirred.

Reaching the first of them, Horner dropped to a knee, rolled the animal over onto its back. It was Allie. Its lifeless eyes were open, lips drawn back, teeth bared, blood trailing from the side of its mouth. Bile rose in Horner's throat as he fought back vomit. He looked down corridor at the others. Lifeless. All of them—when something, Horner saw, was clutched in Allie's hand. Horner started to reach for it.

"Ryan!"

Horner looked up. Adams had moved ahead, was standing in the entrance to the research laboratory. Horner came slowly to his feet. Whatever it was that Adams was staring in at was something not to be seen, he knew. Crossing to Adams, Horner stared with him. In a chair, eyes glazed, staring off at images unknown, sat Enari. At his feet lay Jones' body. On the work table beside the spent .22 were Geronimo's remains, Enari's hand softly caressing its blood matted fur.

DAY FOUR

IN THE HOSPITAL interrogation room, Elinor stared across the desk at Enari. Of all the interviews she'd ever conducted she'd never seen a more shattered man. His eyes were cast down, his hands clutched before him. But she had questions to ask, vital ones.

"Doctor Enari." No response. "Frank. Look at me." His eyes came up, wet and guiless. "Did you know what you were doing?"

"What I was doing?"

"That it was wrong?"

No answer.

"Tell me."

"What?"

"Are you listening to what I'm saying?"

No answer.

"Do you agree or disagree at the time you shot Doctor Jones that it could cause his death?"

"I wasn't thinking anything about shooting him."

"What were you thinking?"

"When I—when it happened—you know like an attack of some kind."

"You felt you were being attacked?"

No answer. But there was. It was on his face. Lines of deep introspection and regret.

"Frank. *Look* at me! It is so important that you understand. A temporary insanity plea is a plea submitted by someone accused of a crime that suggests the defendant was diminished in mental capacity and could not understand the nature or quality of his behavior. Since the condition was temporary, it means the person is no longer insane, but was at the time a crime took place. We're going to try to engage experts to testify—are you listening…?"

"I'm sorry. I'm so sorry. He was my friend. My *friend*." His shoulders began to wrack with guilt. "But I didn't—it didn't—it just happened!"

It had not gone well. The all-night drive alone had been exhausting, Elinor and Aaron sharing time behind the wheel, east across Central Valley, north to Sacramento, then the final thirty miles to the University of California, Davis campus. Phillip Belgano, director of planning and programs at King Hall, the university law school named after Martin Luther King, had set up the meeting, gathered whom he could on short notice. As well as himself, there would be Doctor Roger Hilgarde, forensic psychiatrist, and Doctor Neil St Clair, physician and professor of psychiatry, both from the university's school of medicine, all three noted in their fields, all with classes at nine o'clock. They'd carved out an hour, eight that morning in Belgano's office. A four page single space summary of Elinor's findings had been Faxed ahead, each person present with a copy. Aaron Fogel opened the meeting.

"The enemy is the clock," he said.

"No," Belgano waved the four sides before him in the air. "The enemy is these four pages."

Elinor blanched.

"Could you explain that, please?" she asked.

She felt heat rise. It was clear they'd never heard of her, clear too she would have to show no offense at that. She needed these three, needed them badly. Needed their reputations and testimony.

"He didn't attempt to leave the room?" Belgano was asking.

"The room?"

"Doctor Enari. During your interrogation."

"I don't think so."

"Did he?"

"No."

"He remained in the room."

"Yes."

"He didn't stand mute?"

"Mute?"

"Say nothing?"

"No."

"He responded in some fashion to your questions?"

"Well, let's say he responded. I'm not sure it was always to my questions."

"During your interview."

"Yes."

"So he answered your questions, didn't he?"

"Hardly delusional, grandiose and bizarre," Hilgarde cut in.

"There's a strong case..."

"If one accepts his story."

"But not insane," Belgano concluded.

"Delusional. There were delusions," Elinor pleaded.

"Now in remission, accepting his scenario. Which is the problem," Belgano explained.

"Were there deep roots in his parents tight discipline? Excessive demands and high expectation? Paranoid disorder, pietistic expressions, explosive emotionality?" Hilgarde asked. "No. I've known the man ten years. Nothing of the sort."

"Ultimately a jury will find..." Belgano started to say.

"We don't intend this to go to jury..." Elinor started to say.

"Ultimately a *judge* will find," Belgano corrected himself with some irritation at being interrupted.

"We want a pre-trial hearing to determine an insanity plea," Elinor tried to explain.

"Which, for that to be a legitimate defense in the commission of a crime there must be such a perverted and deranged condition of moral faculties that the defendant, at the time of the commission of the crime was deprived of his memory and understanding and was unable to comprehend the nature of his action."

"Right." It was Hilgarde. "And that is, in fact, a judicial benchmark."

"Yes, but…"

"Further," Belgano went on, "to be unable to distinguish between moral good and evil, or, as is more often stated, to distinguish between right and wrong."

"Still further," Hilgarde interjected, glancing at his watch, "there are those who say, wait a minute, if one shoots a colleague as he admits he has done…"

"Given major depression, psychotic disorders," Elinor pushed her agenda.

"…you should either face the death penalty," Hilgarde overrode her, "or spend the rest of your life behind bars."

"You're saying there's really no other way of looking at this," Aaron cut in.

"The legal standard requires that the defendant be habitually mentally disabled or mentally ill. Is Dr Enari that?' St Clair asked.

"He was."

"At some moment. Perhaps. But not now," Hilgarde insisted.

"If driven by circumstances so extreme…" Elinor defended her conclusions.

"Such as what?" Hilgarde asked. "A psychomotor seizure of episodic decontrol?"

"We don't know that," Belgano argued.

"What we know," Hilgarde concluded, "is that he shot a colleague as well as six monkeys he let loose from their cages, wholly a thing of the moment…'

"That's not what happened."

"You were there? You've a witness?"

"On the other hand," St Claire said, pinching his lower lip with his fingers, "he still can be assessed as having neurotic issues…"

"Some of us walking around the streets of this *campus*…"

Belgano started to say.

"Narcissism is not confined to assassins," Hilgarde finished the thought.

"You have to be crazy to shoot six monkeys," St Clair offered, a ray of hope.

"My problem is from a legal standpoint," Belgano said. "Psychiatry and psychology are soft sciences. There is no exact answer. And in my experience they've been frequently not only wrong but deadly wrong."

"I'm sorry," Hilgarde said, and he seemed to mean it as he looked Elinor over. "But there's a ten ton elephant in the room. Why should we believe a word he's told you. Monkeys running loose? Threatening his life?"

"If he was truthful in his account could it not be postulated events as he encountered them were enough to drive a man to an act of temporary insanity, criminal though it was?" Aaron clung to the point.

"And the proof of that is?" Belgano asked. He looked at Elinor, awaited her reply. There was none.

The ride back was mostly in silence. There'd been talk about staying over, awaiting the group's determination which they'd promised would be forthcoming the following day whether or not to engage as representatives and clinical experts willing to testify on Enari's behalf. Except Elinor had her own court date, nine o'clock the next morning at the Santa Barbara County Court House, and did not want to put it off one day further. It was time to end this marriage. A clean break. Their attorneys had what they needed. Why this face to face encounter was even called for was beyond her. She was not in a fighting mood, not out to squeeze the last dime out of her settlement. Just get it over with and done! And so at nine o'clock the following day she sat on a hard wooden bench in an under-heated assignment room, Judge Norman Haskell presiding.

She looked about. Two dozen others were in the chamber, some huddling with their attorneys, getting last minute instructions before being sent off to courtrooms and destinies unknown.

At ten past nine she saw across the room her lawyer arrive. His name was Harrison Lueck, a name she'd had a difficult time committing to memory. A divorce attorney, recommended by a friend, she'd met him once, spoken to him twice on the phone, found him brusque to the point of irritation.

Dapper, mid-fifties, dressed in sharkskin grey, he came with high credentials, but with a caution, had once been overheard boasting he could seduce any woman he represented in a divorce action. To Elinor's surprise, he carried no brief case, no papers and seemed in a state of agitation. Ignoring Elinor's presence, he turned to a bailiff, seemed, from Elinor's view point, to be pressing the deputy for a response to a question. The bailiff looked over the courtroom, then back to Lueck, shook his head, no. It was not the answer Lueck wanted, Elinor saw, as turning he marched across the room to her.

"Walk with me," he said as he reached her.

"What's wrong?"

"Big trouble. Big trouble."

It should have been a warning and it was. In the corridor Elinor was rushed into a quick step to keep pace as her attorney, her expensive, highly recommended counselor, cursing beneath his breath, surveyed the early morning crush with an expression akin to rage, suddenly spotted whom he was looking for.

"Sam!"

A fellow attorney, files in hand, turned at the sound of his name, Lueck virtually bearding him against the corridor wall.

"You've got me at Warren Barruch's table at the UJA dinner, Goddamnit! I'm not sitting with that son of a bitch!"

On instinct Elinor's heart began to sink. Ten minutes later she discovered her intuition was well placed. Seated at a corner table in the courthouse cafeteria across from her estranged husband and his equally expensive attorney it all came crashing down. For all the pomposity and hostility each lawyer portrayed toward the other, both seemingly elbowing for position, it was quickly apparent neither had done a lick of homework regarding the divorce they'd been hired to negotiate, both bent on bluffing their way through the meeting at combined fees of a thousand dollars an hour, an observation Elinor laid squarely on the table.

"Do either one of you," she asked the attorneys, "have the slightest idea what this settlement entails?"

"If you find my representation inadequate," Leuck huffed with a deliberately dismissive tone.

"I find it non-existent," Elinor answered.

Leuck's mouth snapped open, whatever words he had to say aborted by the sound of Elinor's cell phone. Glancing at the screen she saw the call was from Phillip Belgano, UC Davis.

At five-thirty in the afternoon Elinor dragged herself into her temporary trailer home, closed the door and dropped to the cushioned bench seat. It had become instantly clear to both attorneys that there was little in the way of property and income to be milked in a protracted settlement. There was the house with its hefty mortgage, furnishings, two cars, separate incomes, neither of which projected bountiful fees. The house would be sold, each splitting what might remain of property, bank accounts and assets, balanced on division, credit cards, furnishings auctioned, proceeds if there were any…blah blah blah.

She had tried to keep her mind on the negotiations, tried to recall all they'd agreed to, she couldn't. The phone call had obliterated that.

"Doctor Barry?"

"Yes."

"Phil Belgano."

"Yes."

"I'm sorry."

All the rest that followed, how they'd struggled with decision, not easy to make considering Frank Enari was a colleague, but, no, they were sorry, it was unanimous, their decision endorsed by a restatement of what had been discussed the day before, the difficulty in believing his account of events—she barely heard any of what followed, only the obligatory ending, "We wish you luck," as the phone went dead.

She drew in a deep breath. She had a call to make, She'd avoided it. Through the divorce proceedings, lunch, resumed negotiations, sitting in her car unmoving once all was concluded, the drive back to Goleta. She picked up her cell phone and dialed. Aaron Fogel answered on the first ring.

"Elinor?

"Yeah."

The "Yeah" said it all.

"Jesus. What happened?"

"They don't believe him."

"What don't they believe?"

"His story."

"Which part?

"All of it. They think the two of them got into it."

"Into it. What're they talking about?"

"They didn't want to speculate. Forced to they said the two had been known to have a quarrelsome relationship from time to time at the University, Enari especially, mostly on theories. Something, given the altitude, probably triggered a conflict."

"What about the monkeys?"

"They feel he released them as a cover."

"A cover."

"The terror of them supposedly driving him to an act of insanity."

There was a long pause on the other end of the line.

"Aaron?"

"What do *you* think," he asked at length.

"I've gone over it fifty times. I've reviewed our meetings, analyzed his responses and reactions to my questions, his body language, demeanor." She paused. "I believe him, Aaron."

"Believe him? Or want to believe him?"

Another pause.

"What?" she asked.

"What other scenario could there be?" Aaron said.

"Other than?"

"His letting the monkeys out."

She had no answer, settled on, "What's next?"

"He's been transferred back to Inyo County,"

"Independence?" she asked.

"Right."

"When'd that happen?"

"This afternoon," Aaron said. "The Grand Jury there will hear from the D.A. An indictment's a forgone conclusion. He'll be assigned a Public Defender. Probably go for a plea. Temporary insanity's out, given what you've just told me. Without his colleagues supporting his testimony, I don't know what he's got."

It was Elinor's turn to be silent.

"Elinor?"

"Still here."

"Look, you were brought in to make an assessment. You did that to your best. I can sense how you feel about it. You did your job, it's the most you can do. You've got your life to get back to. Send in a statement of billable hours and don't short yourself. They'll scream, but you'll get it."

There was more, shared sympathy, compliments, then he was gone.

It was 6:45, grown dark, before Elinor realized she had been sitting immobilized in the dark, staring into space for an hour, beset by stress and failures of the day. She snapped on the light, unraveled slowly, both body and mind, thought about dinner, passed on the thought, not hungry, looked about the trailer, barren and cold. She had been advised early on not to remove anything that might be in contention from the house she shared with her husband till the divorce settlement was completed, had brought only clothes, some personals, and a box of treasured books, which stood at the end of the bench. She glanced at them. One, which caught her attention, stood atop the pile. St Catherine's High School Bulletin, Commencement issue. She picked it up, opened it.

Inside the cover was the requisite listing of staff, a photograph of the year's valedictorian, along with the school's mission statement.

"Through commitment, scholarship, companionship and service, each member of St Catherine's community…"

She turned to the table of contents. Headmaster's Address. Student Commencement Address. Baccalaureate Addresses, of which there were two, Elinor's one of them. She flipped through the pages to the Year End Commencement Awards. Her name was listed on three, one Faculty Recognition, two Academic. Through more pages to Advisory Comments, each graduating student listed with their class picture, found hers, and beside it in italics, *High Honors.* Below, as with each, was a personalized character summary.

"Elinor came to St Catherine's in her junior year on full scholarship, and quickly won friends and admirers from a community that gravitates to compassionate, curious people. Graduating with high honors she used psychology the way others might use oils or pastels, rending truth in her creative and innovate ways. As a co-Baccalaureate addressee her topic, how unproductive and unenlightened societal roles are perpetuated, left us realizing truths we had not previously appreciated, demonstrating, to those watching and listening, what never ending inquiry and engagement look like."

She stared at that paragraph, reading and rereading it, trying to recall the girl who'd inspired it. "Never ending inquiry and engagement."

She lowered the issue, sat contemplating. Coming to decision, she quickly rose, sought out her overnight suitcase, opened it.

DAY FIVE

IT WAS THREE O'CLOCK in the morning that Elinor drove her Prius into Independence, county seat of the eastern Sierra Inyo County, elevation 3930 feet, population 669 on the roadside sign flashing by as she entered the town. She'd called ahead to its several motels before she found the Winnedumah B&B that had a vacancy, a tight squeeze this time of year, the opening month of trout season. The seven hour drive through the night had been exhausting. She'd texted Aaron where she was going not wanting to phone, knowing he'd try to talk her out if it, tried to keep her mind on where she was going, and why, kept alert by a sandwich and cups of thick black coffee at Mike's Roadhouse Cafe in Mojave where she refilled her car.

If the Grand Jury could be made to accept Dr Enari's state of mind at the time of the homicide, especially considering his terror of and ultimate encounter with the monkeys, they might be brought around to consider finding that he had acted in a state of extreme emotional disturbance, though temporary, she reasoned, and that this disturbance had a reasonable explanation. The strategy in that regard might well influence the Grand Jury, she hoped, by the relative consequences of the possible verdicts…

But bats darting in and out of her headlights as she headed north on US 395 through Red Rock Canyon, past Little Rock, Olancha and Lone Pine, the towering snow-capped Sierras rising eerily in moonlight diverted concentration. Further fishermen on their way to just-opened streams and lakes impatiently blinked their brights, bullying her to move over, out of the way as they raced past her in their SUV's and pickups on the two lane highway.

True to its promise, a night clerk was waiting at the Winnedumah as Elinor drove in across a snow-fed creek, suffered through a full explanation of the B&B's amenities and was shown to a basic country-style single. A printed brochure by the bed announced, "Whether it's your honeymoon, anniversary, special event or just a chance to get away, our warm and friendly staff…"

Dropping her overnight to the floor, she threw off her clothes down to brassiere and panties, set her travel alarm for seven, fell onto the bed uncovered and succumbed to fitful sleep.

As all courthouses in California, Inyo County's in Independence opened for business at eight in the morning, an elaborately designed neo-classical three story built in the twenties, as out of place in this Sierra wide spot in the trail as its most infamous visitor, Charles Manson.

"Sheriff's Station," Elinor was told at reception. "Jail's at the Sheriff's Station."

"Which is?"

"South Clay Street."

A two minute drive brought her to her destination, a low-lying single story bunker-like concrete windowless building. The Desk Sergeant confirmed Doctor Enari had been brought in the day before and was being held pending Grand Jury disposition.

"I'd like to see him," Elinor explained.

"You are?" The Sergeant was in his fifties, ruddy complexioned, gnarled hands.

She gave her name and her association with the prisoner.

"Visiting hours with prisoners are Saturday and Sunday," the Sergeant explained. "Nine to four. Reservations for visits can be made the day of visits between eight to two."

It was Thursday. She would have to wait two days.

"Is there any way to expedite that?" she asked.

He studied her a moment.

"Wait here, please."

Five minutes later he returned with a civilian-suited man, mid-thirties, Paiute Indian ancestry, Elinor guessed, short, squat, muscular, hair cut close, face wide and open, but seasoned, with an aptitude for dealing with the burdensome.

"Mrs Barry?" he said in greeting.

"*Doctor* Barry," she corrected.

"Doctor. Sorry. I'm Philip Moon, with the District Attorney's office. How can I help you?"

"You've a prisoner, here. Doctor Frank Enari. Just brought in, as I understand. I'd like to see him."

"You were assigned as psychiatric investigator of Doctor Enari when he was at Santa Rita, I understand?"

"I was."

"And your reason for being here now?"

"Give it any name you want. Amicus Curiae, if that fits. I want to see him."

"Doctor Enari is currently undergoing interrogation."

"He was interrogated when he was brought down from the mountain."

"Superficially and without response."

"Who's in there with him now? His lawyer?"

"Doctor Enari has been assigned a public defender. He's waived his rights to have him present."

"That's crazy. Look, I don't know what's going on. I want to be there!"

"I'm afraid I can't accommodate that. If I may suggest an alternative."

The room was dark, small, no more than ten by twelve. Four swivel chairs faced a wall-length one-way viewing glass. Seated in one of the viewing chairs, the youthful prosecutor beside her, Elinor looked in on an interrogation room, Enari, dressed in prison blues, seated at a plain metal table. All the life, she saw, seemed to have drained out of him. His responses to the Detective across the table from him were flat and sterile, conversation between the two picked up in the one way viewing room through a speaker.

"Okay, let's review," the Detective was saying, his inquiries mannerly, not hostile. "An incident happened on the mountain, right?"

"Yes."

"Okay. And the incident we've been discussing resulted in the death of your partner."

"Yes."

"Doctor Robert Jones."

"Yes."

"Is that right?"

"Yes."

"Shot by you, is that correct?"

"Yes."

"With a twenty-two automatic."

"I don't know what it was."

"Okay. Was it, was it in reference to something Doctor Jones had done?"

"No."

"You were not mad at Doctor Jones?"

"No."

"Okay. You had thoughts of doing this prior to that day?

"No."

"How long had you been having thoughts about wanting or not wanting to kill him."

"It just happened."

"That day."

"Yes."

"Was he sitting down or standing?"

"Standing."

"When you shot him."

"Yes."

"Okay. Was there a struggle?"

"No."

"Was he trying to run from you?"

"No."

"Was there talk between you?"

"Yes."

"Okay. About what?"

"The monkeys."

"The monkeys."

"Yes."

"That you and Doctor Jones were assigned to work with."

"Yes."

"What did he say?"

"He said they were trying to kill us."

"The monkeys. Trying to kill you." The doubt in his voice was impossible to mask.

"Yes."

"Those were his words?"

"I don't remember his words."

"Okay. But that's what you heard?"

"Yes."

"Or thought you heard."

"Yes."

"That's when you shot him?

"Yes."

"Because you were afraid of what he was saying?"

"Yes."

"About the monkeys."

"Yes."

"Then why would you release them from their cages."

"I didn't."

"They just got out on their own."

"I don't know how they got out."

"Okay. They were out. They were coming for you, you said."

"Yes."

"So you shot them too."

"Yes."

"Doctor Jones, then the monkeys."

"Yes."

"Because you thought they were going to kill you."

"Yes."

"Okay. Are you aware there's a great deal of illogic to what you've just told me?"

"It's what happened."

"That you are opening yourself up with this confession not only to a charge of murder but also the maximum penalty in this case?"

In the viewing room Elinor reached forward snapped off the audio. She sat a moment. Her face was stone.

"I want to see his lawyer," she said.

The Desk Sergeant checked his blotter. "Harold Taverner. 617 Main Street, Bishop. I have his phone if you'd like."

"That would be helpful."

He wrote the information down, gave it to her. She thanked him, turned to leave.

"I'd be on notice, Ma'am…"

She looked back at him. It was clear from his expression he had something further he wanted to say, thought better of it, settled on, "617 Main Street."

In her car she sat a moment, heat pressing in on her brain. Where had his attorney *been*? Not there, no one there to caution Enari with his answers which, from her perspective, one by one, pounded nails in his coffin. She looked at the name, address and phone number of the Public Defender the Sergeant had given her. Harold Taverner, Main Street, Bishop, forty miles up 395. She took out her cell phone, dialed the number, was met with a recording. The office was currently closed, would be open at eleven, please leave a message. Eleven. Not a bustling enterprise.

Sounding as urgent as possible, she replied, left her name and reason for wanting to meet, was on her way up from Independence, would be there in less than an hour. She closed the phone. But one thing lingered, what she'd heard from the Desk Sergeant as she left, or hadn't heard, that he'd seemed to want to tell her, but had decided against it. What, she didn't know, but was beginning to sense she did. Frank Enari was being abandoned. And worse, was abandoning himself. She set her car into gear, steered it onto the highway.

Bishop, compared to Independence, was a metropolis. A town of nearly four thousand, it was the largest in the Eastern Sierra south of Reno. Bait and tackle shops along the main artery, Main Street, were doing land office business, day and half-day fishing guides advertised for hire, lakes and streams. Locals raced souped-up hot rods, pipes rapping, up and back the mile long Main, into and back through the town. Number 617, she found, was located mid-town, a two-story stucco, tenants advertised, among them Harold Taverner, Attorney-At-Law, Criminal and DUI Defense, suite 206.

Climbing the steps to his second floor office Elinor glanced at her watch, It was eleven-fifteen. Her pulse was racing. She opened the door, entered a modest reception. A secretary turned from making coffee at a hot plate. She was, Elinor saw, in her sixties, old fashioned dress, proved to be loquacious, attentive. A name plate on her desk read "Mrs Reed."

"Hi," she greeted Elinor warmly.

"Hello," Elinor answered.

"You're the one called in?"

"I am."

"Coffee?"

Elinor hesitated, then, "Sure."

"You on that murder thing?" Mrs Reed asked.

"I beg your pardon?"

"Up on the mountain."

"Murder thing?"

"Biggest thing to hit the county since Manson."

Elinor nodded. Manson. "I'd like to see Mr Taverner, if I could."

"Give him ten minutes," Mrs Reed said. "Wednesday's Rotary. Cream?"

"Black's fine."

"I was fifteen. Sixteen? Fifteen," Mrs Reed remembered. "They found Manson at the Goler Wash on the Barker Ranch out in Panamint Valley. Caught him hiding under a bathroom vanity in one of the abandoned shacks. Just drop his name here aparts it's akin to mentioning that Ripper fellow in London. People think they brought him in on the murder charges. They didn't know about the murders, not at first, they didn't, not till the L.A. people came up. At first, didn't have a clue what they had, brought him in for vandalism and stealing a dune buggy."

Elinor had taken the coffee from Mrs Reed with a "Thank you," turned to the window overlooking the street, drawn to the rapping pipes below, looked down on the hotrods racing up and down when her cell phone went off. Digging it from her purse, she glanced at its phone window. Aaron Fogel. She snapped it closed, not answering the call, would get back to him later.

"Trolling Main," Mrs Reed was explaining.

"I beg your pardon?"

"S'what the kids call it. Mile up street to the end of town, then back. Trolling Main. Not much else to do if it isn't fishing or making out at Convict Lake."

Elinor nodded in perfunctory understanding. 'Making out.' When' was the last time she heard *that* one, when the door opened and Harold Taverner entered from the stairs. Dressed in brown suit, white shirt, string tie, coat slung over his shoulder, he was in his late sixties, still clinging to what legal work came his way so long as it didn't keep him up at nights. Taking no initial notice of Elinor he faced Mrs Reed who'd returned to her desk.

"Carl Benefiel and his damn snow pack talks. God, the man can go on." he said with a shake of his head. "Calls?"

"There's the decision from the State Appeals Court. Refused to consider."

Taverner nodded, accepting defeat as common place.

"And they want you on the Borycki hit and run."

"No ex-cons." He looked up, caught Elinor's stare.

"I'm Doctor Elinor Barry," Elinor stepped forward, hand outstretched in greeting, aborting Mrs Reed's introduction. "I'm a forensic therapist. I was engaged to interview Doctor Enari at Santa Rita while he was there. I'd like to talk to you about that, if I could."

Through the years Elinor had become expert at reading expressions. Harold Taverner's, she saw, said it all. She was being regarded with great suspicion.

"Come on in," he said.

Taverner's office, she quickly saw, was a testament to his modest history. There were the obligatory desk photos of children and grandchildren. On shelves, between an equally obligatory array of law books, were framed certificates, a BA from San Francisco State and a law degree from Glendale Law School which she'd never heard of, as well as plaques acknowledging local civic services. There was another plaque too, a five pound rainbow trout occupying one wall, a gag, with lettering beneath it reading, "The One That Got Away."

Draping his coat over the back of his chair, Taverner dropped into it, stared across his desk as Elinor took a seat. It was clear he was waiting for her to open the meeting.

"I've just come up from Independence where Doctor Enari's being held. I'm told you've been assigned to represent him."

Taverner hesitated, a wary fox. He gestured acknowledgment with a slight wave of one finger.

"He's undergoing interrogation," Elinor continued, fighting for control. "With a right to have an attorney present. None is."

"Doctor Enari has chosen not to contest the charges against him."

"When was that decided."

"When he was brought in."

"Under whose advice?"

Taverner sat back slowly, as though placing distance from an adversary.

"What is it you want?" he asked

"You're pleading nolo contendere. No contest."

"I'm trying to save your man from a lethal injection."

"How're you going to deal with that?" She was growing combative, tried to control it. She couldn't.

"I'm not *dealing* with anything."

"Apparently not."

Taverner's face flushed with color. She saw the veins in his neck were throbbing and he was sweating.

"So you're saying well, he did this, the target of evil forces," Taverner answered, deflecting with evasion.

"I'm saying the man was driven to an uncontrollable act of temporary insanity…"

"Crazed by a pack of murderous monkeys."

"Yes."

"Which is what he told you."

"Yes."

"Shifting from topic to topic," Taverner went on with rising sarcasm, the lawyer to a hostile witness, "with no obvious connection, providing excessive and irrelevant detail? Is that what you witnessed?"

"That is *not* what I witnessed."

"So what he needs to do is go to a shrink for a few months and put him back in society."

"Not society, no…"

"Wiping tears from his eyes saying, 'Don't fret, don't cry, you're a sick, sick boy.'"

"He belongs in a controlled environment for treatment, not prison."

"Well, that monkey stuff. I kind of think ol' Frank just went off his rocker and got mad and wanted to shoot somebody. Call it a rupture of the ego. That ain't diminished capacity, insanity, temporary or otherwise. Nobody's going to swallow it. You take that to the Grand Jury…"

"I want to try."

"And tell them what? That this is all about a pack of monkeys driving him mad? They not only won't believe you, they'll hate you."

"So all you want to do is slide."

The muscles in Taverner's face tightened to the point of rupture. She wondered briefly if he might have a heart attack. He pushed back from his desk and rose.

"Thank you for coming, Doctor Barry. Let me see you to the door."

Returned to her Prius, Elinor sat, motor on, heater on. With a sudden burst of frustration she slammed her fists against the steering wheel, fought back tears when the cell phone sounded again from her purse. It was Aaron, she saw, Aaron again, her first instinct to ignore the call. Thinking better of it, she opened the phone.

"Yes, Aaron."

"Where are you?"

"Bishop. Just talked to his lawyer."

"Okay, listen…"

"Waste of time. I should have taken the guy to the floor."

"Elinor…"

"Didn't have the guts."

"*Elinor!*"

"What?"

"I got a call. There's somebody there wants to talk to you."

"No press, forget it."

"That's not what this is."

"Who?"

"You got a pen?"

"Come on, Aaron. What are we doing?" she said irritably.

"You're going to want to talk to him. I've got his number."

He gave her the name which at first meant nothing, then, with slow recall, did. A chill went through her. Finding a Visa receipt from her dinner purchase in Mojave, she turned it over to its blank back side, pulled a pen from her purse.

"Give me the number," she said.

Six miles north of Bishop Elinor found the turn out. White Mountain Road. She slowed as she reached it, arriving at a rusting roadside sign riddled with bullet holes, stared at a deserted two lane asphalt running east across the upper Owens Valley, seemingly into oblivion toward a range that formed the eastern wall of the Valley. At first she tried to assess if in fact she'd accurately committed the instructions she'd written so hastily. There was no sign of life, no buildings, nothing. She looked at her scrawled directions again. White Mountain Road. Turn east, eight miles. Again she looked down the road. With no alternative, she took it.

High desert, volcanic, wildflowers, after a somewhat disappointingly dry spring, were trying to make the best of it. Sagebrush were carpeted with yellow flowered buckwheat and wild white phlox. Occasional clumps of lupine fought their way through hard packed soil. Yet in all that mighty sweep of land she saw no sign of man, nor the handiwork of man. She flung a measuring glance at the clouding sky, drawn to it by a cacophony of honking when she saw it. Flying in a V pattern no more than a hundred feet off the ground, a flight of Canadian Geese were returning to their summer homes fifteen hundred miles to the north. She slowed to a near stop, mesmerized by what she was seeing, lowered her driver's side window the better to hear till they were gone leaving behind not a sigh of wind, only the air, drowsy with its weight of flowering perfume. Raising the window, she accelerated, crossed the Owens River and was jarred from her reverie where the asphalt surface gave way to dirt.

It was three miles further on that she saw it ahead in the distance, the network of low-lying buildings. Approaching, the first to catch her attention was the helicopter on its concrete pad outside its aluminum housing. Workers were unloading boxes from its cargo bay. Fifty yards further on she came to the sign:

HEADQUARTERS
TOWER MOUNTAIN RESEARCH STATION
ELEVATION 4,100

Turning in, she drew to a stop before a building designated "Office." For a long moment she sat, contemplating her surroundings, grown suddenly bleak as clouds erased the sun. She reached for the door handle to exit the car, drew back startled at the loud rapping on her window glass, stared into the face of a bearded man she'd never met but had come to know.

"Ryan Horner," he said, opening her door. He was younger than she'd expected, earnest, which she had, but filled with an anguish she hadn't prepared for but should have. Looking her over he said in greeting, "You're going to want some heavy weather gear."

Twenty minutes later, dressed in ankle-length coat, plastic boots to her knees, Elinor sat strapped in the back of the helicopter alongside Horner, Val Adams at the controls. The liftoff had been seamless, the climb unbuffetted by lack of wind, the melted snow below risen and rising to an ungainly line across the terrain.

She glanced across at Horner. He had virtually said nothing, told her nothing since her arrival, only that he had something to show her. Whatever it was, what he meant, he had yet to explain, other than she was to join him in the helicopter. That was it, nothing more. But his face, she saw, his jaw thrust out, lips tightly pursed, portrayed an emotion she couldn't detect.

The flight, unencumbered by weather, was brief, Summit Laboratory coming into view in its notch below the brooding cover of Tower Mountain, the helicopter circling once about the laboratory, then settling on its pontoons to a makeshift pad stamped out of hard-packed snow. A plowed corridor had been shoveled from the pad to the building's entrance where, she saw, boxes taped and numbered stood awaiting shipment.

Once inside Elinor found it much as she'd imagined from Enari's description, though not enough to prepare her for the sight of scattered blood-stained patches in the corridor. Blood coagulates, turns plastic-like, she knew, when left to dry. Efforts had been made to scoop it up with spatulas. But stains remained. Otherwise, she saw, the place was barren, nearing empty, two workmen boxing all that was portable as Horner led her into the kitchen-common room. The furniture remained, as did the stove, refrigerator and short wave radio. Coffee, stale and steaming, stood on a low burner on the stove. There was no sound other than the hum of the generator on low, providing flickering light. Gratefully heat was on, servicing the building.

"You can get rid of that," Horner gestured at her coat.

Crossing to the stove he poured two cups of coffee, turned to the kitchen table, set one mug before him, pushed the other across for her. Shedding herself of her all weather coat, Elinor followed him to the table.

"What do you know about what happened here?" he asked.

She looked at him. In the flickering light she saw what she could not detect on the helicopter. It was despair. And why not. The man had lost everything, everything and all of importance to him.

"I know what I was told," she answered, seating herself across from him.

"Given that, what is it you hope to accomplish?"

She studied him a moment more, metaphorically holding her breath. Till now she'd asked no questions, made no inquiries, uncertain what he wanted of her.

"I want to establish an insanity defense for Doctor Enari," she said. "Prison's preposterous. Though his actions were criminal, by reason of mental illness he cannot fairly be held responsible for those actions."

"The M'Naghten standard."

"A fixture in Anglo-American law," she answered, surprised he'd heard of it.

"Which leads you where?"

"Under normal circumstances?"

"Assuming."

"To inquire if Doctor Enari has an abnormal and damaged brain," she went on. "For this we have two types of objective data, entirely independent of each other. Psychological tests which can be faked, and an EEG for abnormal brain waves which can't."

"You think that's what you have here?"

Elinor seemed to hold her breath before answering, this time for real, sat back.

"No," she admitted.

'So where are you?"

"I don't think he knew what he was getting into. I think they were left here, even after the discovery of Vogel, not knowing what they'd find."

"And?"

"I think the revelation by Doctor Jones that the monkeys were doing to them, what they were doing to the monkeys, as clearly had happened to Vogel before them, so terrified Doctor Enari, it drove him to an act of dementia. I think, meaning only to ward off Jones with the gun he'd found, he fired involuntarily to stop what he was hearing, only to find that Jones had it right as he saw the monkeys coming on."

"An act of irresistible impulse."

"Numerous courts have recognized that an insanity plea included the inability to control one's actions, despite knowing such actions were wrong—though how those animals escaped their cages…"

"Letting them loose himself as a cover?" Horner postulated.

"That seems to be what everyone believes. Or wants to believe. Which, without proof he had nothing to do with it, no jury would accept it as a defense."

"But you don't believe it was Enari." Horner said.

"Given his fear and state of mind it would, in *his* mind, have been suicidal."

Horner took a long sip from his coffee, set it back on the table, nodded.

"You're correct."

Whatever Elinor expected Horner to say that wasn't it.

"I beg your pardon?" she said.

"He did not release the monkeys."

She stared, incredulous.

"You can't know that. You weren't here."

"I wasn't here, but I know who did."

It was seconds before she recovered enough to ask.

"Who? There was no one else here but Doctor Jones."

"Yes, there was."

A chill ran through Elinor. "You're scaring the hell out of me," she said.

Horner pushed back his chair, rose to his feet.

"Come on."

Following Horner the length of the corridor, side-stepping the blood stains, Elinor was brought to the examination and housing room where the monkeys had been held. The cage doors stood open, cages empty. The keys to the cages remained as always, attached to a ring, hung on a wall well out of reach of the cages.

"This," Horner explained as they entered, "is where the monkeys were quartered. Six of them. Each in his own cage, each cage locked. They were fed through these narrow trap openings in their doors, were only brought out under sedation."

"Who let them out?" Elinor asked.

"They let themselves out," Horner answered.

She stared at him in disbelief and confusion.

"How? The keys to the cages are half way across the room."

"Those keys are. There are always two sets. When Val Adams found Vogel frozen to death in the electronics room Vogel's keys were missing, and never found. Adams said so. He'd radioed that. It was assumed Vogel lost them outside when shoveling snow. It was a wrong assumption."

Reaching into his pocket he withdrew a ring of keys which he deposited on an examination table. "When I arrived with Adams to find Jones and the monkeys shot to death, one of the monkeys, Allie, was clutching these in his fist."

Elinor stared at the keys, stunned.

"How did he get them?"

"Carelessness, inattention on Vogel's part," Horner speculated. "Monkeys weren't picked for this project because they were stupid. They were picked because they were closest to man. Which was my mistake."

"I'm out of the office at the moment or with a patient. Leave a message and I will get back to you as soon as I can."

In her car, re-crossing the Owens River, approaching the main north-south 395, Elinor gripped her cell phone in frustration. It was the third time she'd tried to reach Aaron Fogel at Santa Rita Hospital since landing back at the Research Station, and it was the third time she'd gotten his recording.

"Aaron. Elinor, again. Listen, this is vital. Set up a meeting with the people at Davis again. Soon as you can. Horner's available to attend. He's got what they asked for. I'm heading down to Independence to see Enari. This is an incredible break, no guarantee, but hope. Supposedly I'm not allowed to see prisoners till Saturday. I'm going to bull my way through that. Call me soon as you can."

She snapped closed her phone, slowed as she reached the main highway, saw it clear, turned south, headed through Bishop on her way to Independence. It was just the beginning, she knew. Juries, Grand or otherwise, *hated* the insanity plea. But Horner's recounting of events was so gripping, so shocking and bizarre, she felt there was more than an even chance the experts at Enari's university could be brought aboard for corroborating testimony...

The siren jarred her out of her thoughts. She looked in the rear view mirror. Red lights were coming fast. She glanced at her speedometer. Eighty-five! Oh, God. All she needed. She slowed, started to pull to the side of the road, when no police at car all, but an ambulance roared past. Gripping the wheel, bare knuckle white, she waited for her pulse to recede, gathered her breath, slowly regained the highway, locking the speedometer in at fifty-five, tried to re-gather her thoughts. Where was she? Horner. How much of his testimony would be intelligible and meaningful to experts, not to mention whose experts, let alone jurors who heard it? It had convinced *her* and it hadn't started out that way. Still suppose...

She tried to shake off doubts. One thing at a time. First Earni. Then Aaron. Then Davis, with Horner

Twenty minutes later she pulled into the parking area at the Independence Sheriff's Station. The ambulance that had passed her, she saw, was parked there, too. Entering, Elinor found the reception empty, other than the Desk Sergeant she'd seen hours before.

"I know it's not Saturday," she met the officer head on. "I want to see Doctor Enari. I'll be ten minutes, that's all. I know you can't authorize that on your own, but that young prosecutor I was talking to can."

The Desk Sergeant held on her a moment, an exceptionally long one she sensed. He picked up his phone.

END OF DAY FIVE

IT WAS JUST PAST SEVEN that night that Elinor arrived at her temporary hilltop home just north of Santa Barbara. The dogs, she saw, were in the house. Taking the path to her trailer, she found a note attached to the door. Removing it, she unlocked the door, stepped inside, turned on the light, glanced at the note.

"Hey!" it read. "Happy days! Where are you? Come on up to the house when you're back, drink a toast to your settlement, dumping that son of a bitch." It was signed, "Orchid."

She set the note alongside her overnight bag, reached into her purse, pulled out a photograph, stared at it.

They take this photograph, the thought went through her mind. A Polaroid. But it's blurred. Still you see the wires and tubes. He's patched into some central mechanical mother, compressors, pumps, brought in by the ambulance's paramedics. There's a tube down his throat, but all too late. They'd taken away his shoe laces and belt. But they hadn't taken away the plastic bag they handed him when he arrived with tooth brush, tooth paste, soap and comb. Suicide by asphyxiation, not hanging, they hadn't anticipated that, a plastic bag over his head. Now they've got this photograph all fuzzy, because someone who's been taking pictures a thousand years decided, just decided, it's going to look nicer, not too gruesome in the papers if he jiggled his hand just a bit as he lifted the shutter, showing their efforts to revive, despite the fact the man was long gone.

She lowered the Polaroid to the table, picked up the note from Orchid again, thought a moment, took out her cell phone, dialed. Orchid's voice came on the line.

"Hey!"

"That invitation still on?" Elinor asked.

"Got to sing for your supper."

"You won't believe what you're going to hear. I don't know whose attorney was worse, my husband's or mine."

"Over cocktails."

"See you."

She closed her cell phone, gave the Polaroid one final look, found herself unable to hold back an involuntary sob.

"Oh, God, oh, God, oh, God," she cried with heartbreaking despair.

She shook her head, steadied herself, rose, crossed to the door, opened it, turned off the light, stepped into the night. The dogs had been let out and ran to greet her.

"Hey, guys," she said, patting each. The house lights were fully on for her now, she saw. Crickets were doing their thing. She wondered if, in their short time on earth, they were ruled by psychotic disorder. She shook it off, climbed the path toward the house.

THE END